The Plague

Civilization's Near Self-Destruction

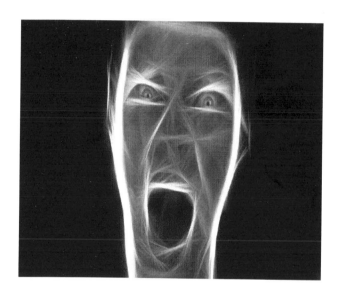

Science Fiction

by
Don Lubov

Lindon Publishing
Summerfield, FL 34491

Website: www.donlubov.com

ISBN - 13: 978-1720386537
ISBN - 10: 1720386536

Books in Print

Near Death in the Gila National Forest (memoir)

An End to Stress – A Guru's Guide to Inner Peace (self-help)

The Side Job (novel)

The Writers Bloc Club (anthology)

Frosty the Soulman (picture book)

Dedication

To my wife, Linda

Acknowledgements

Joe Goldstein

Gwen Rutter

LuAnn Erlich

The Plague

Civilization's Near Self-Destruction

Science Fiction

By
Don Lubov

"Anger is an acid that can do more harm to the vessel in which it is stored than to anything on which it is poured." Mark Twain

The Plague
(2040 AD)

All events presented here are as reported by Dave Miller, of the Daily Chronicle, and his grandson, Reggie Miller, of Channel 3 News

"If the plague hadn't arrived that morning, it would have been a day like any other. People would go to work or school or play and expect life to continue much as it had for as long as anyone could remember."

* * *

"Dave. Stop dawdling. Stop fidgeting with your tie. Your sweater looks fine. Your pants look fine. Your hair is neat. For God's sake, stop wasting time. Nat's waiting for you at the newspaper. Blake is expecting you, too. What is your assignment now, anyway?"

"There have been an unusual series of plane crashes in the last few days."

"Where? asks Dave's wife, Sharon?"

"All over the U.S. Strangest thing anyone's ever seen." Blake is covering it and, as usual, I'm tagging along."

"When you say it like that, it sounds like you don't like playing second fiddle to Blake."

"Sharon, you know that's not true. Blake has taught me more about journalism than I could have learned in college. He's my mentor. I appreciate everything he's shown me. It's just that I'd like the chance to write for the paper on my own. I'd like to have my own byline…Dave Miller, reporter. It has a nice ring to it."

"Patience my dear. Blake has always supported you and, you know he likes you. I'm sure you'll get your chance to make your own mark at the paper, soon."

"You're right, of course. Okay, I'm on my way. Good luck at the lab. I'll see you for dinner. I love you."

"I love you, too, Dave."

*   *   *

Week 1

"Welcome to Flight 105, non-stop to New York. Our crew is ready to serve you. Our Service-bots are also here to serve you. Please place your 'float-bags' in the overhead storage compartments, and take your seats as quickly as you can. We will be departing shortly."

"Marie, if you demo the seat belts, I'll tend to any special requests. Okay?"

Marie, a former beauty queen, can't help but make the other stewardesses look less attractive. Her custom-tailored uniform only adds to the differences.

"Sure…and Dana, thanks for helping out today."

"My pleasure. Any opportunity to be of service."

Dana, a modestly attractive 35-year old, is flying today even though she's not scheduled for this flight. She can't help but notice the quiet interplay between Marie and the captain.

"Morning, Captain. All rested for our flight?"

Marie gently touches the captain's arm as he walks to the cockpit. Captain John Frasier, tall and tan, briefly caresses Marie's hand.

*   *   *

"So, Marie, how's it going with the captain?"

"Why, whatever do you mean? You know the captain's married. I would never get involved with a married man. Besides, Dana, what makes you think the captain would play around?"

"Oh, just a suspicion." *Do I think the captain plays around? You better believe it. How do I know? That's none of your business. Don't you worry, Miss Beauty Queen, your day is coming. Very soon.*

Following the usual protocol, the 10 crew members and 7 Bots ready all 524 passengers on the Jumbo Jet for departure. Pillows and blankets are handed out and, as requested by some, Drowse-pills are provided. Some of the early arrivals are already asleep; their Drowse-pills having taken effect in seconds. Some children are fidgeting in their seats. A baby cries. A Fly-bot approaches the baby and offers an electric, 'Neuro-pacifier'. The baby's mother holds out her arm to be swiped by the 'Bot' and receives the pacifier. The baby sucks, and within seconds, is asleep.

Marie grabs coffee for three and heads for the cockpit. A few minutes later, the announcement to buckle up for take-off comes, but Marie is not in her seat."

Sandy, always a stickler for rules, says: "Where is Marie? She should be here for the take off. That's the protocol. She better be seated properly, somewhere."

The takeoff is smooth and the weather accommodating. Everything is as it should be. Captain Frasier turns over the controls to his co-pilot, Greg, and heads for the lounge.

"Hi Captain. What brings you back here with us underlings?"

"You know I don't consider the crew underlings. I think of you more as my family. Has anyone seen Marie? And where's Dana?"

Jamie, the newest and youngest member of the crew says: "I saw Marie in the galley a minute ago. I don't know where Dana is."

"Thanks, Jamie, I'll check there."

No Marie here. No Dana. Strange, how do you get lost on a plane?

The Captain looks in the galley and the lounge. He looks on both decks to no avail.

I'll check the head.

"Dammit, what's the matter with this door? It won't open all the way." The captain puts his shoulder to the small door and gives a mighty shove. The door opens just enough for him to peer in.

"Aaarrgh! No! Oh, God! Somebody help. Marie, no. Please be alright."

Marie is not all right. Her throat's been slit and she's bled out in the head. The captain grabs the intercom to call his co-pilot.

"Greg. Come in, Greg."

Strange, there's no answer.

The captain rushes to the cockpit to call the authorities. As he opens the cockpit door, he sees Greg's bloody body, slumped over the controls.

"What the hell is going on? Dana, what are you doing here?"

"You shouldn't have dumped me for Marie!" shrieks Dana, as she plunges her laser-knife into the captain's belly. "I'm better than ten Maries!"

The captain slumps to the floor. Dana disengages the autopilot and, her rage spent, hugs the captain, as they plunge from cruising altitude.

"There, there." she says, while stroking the captain's thick, gray hair. "It'll all be over soon."

Dana expires, collapses and shrivels up before the doomed plane hits the ground. There's no one present to detect the horrific odor in the cockpit.

*   *   *

"Where have you been? I called you three times. N-never mind. You're here. That's all that matters. Dave, this is serious. I wouldn't c-call you at work if there weren't something strange going on here. I want you to look into it."

Dave Miller, the preppy-looking, neat-freak, investigative reporter with the Daily Chronicle, stares at his wife, Sharon. She's not the type to get rattled for no reason, and she's obviously frantic now.

"I've been investigating a series of plane crashes for the newspaper. I told you that this morning. Sharon, honey, I've never seen you like this. You're scaring me. Please, calm down, dear, and tell me what's stressing you out."

"Calm? You want calm?... screams Sharon. We'll see how calm you are when I show you what's been going on."

"See", she yells, pointing to the body on the gurney. "Do you see this body? Do you see how emaciated it is? And that smell. My God, Dave, this body smells putrid. I have five more just like it over there, and six more like it out in the hall. This is not normal. My morgue is swamped. This needs to be investigated. Now!"

Shaking and pacing back and forth, Sharon stares at the bodies on the gurneys as Dave studies them.

"Don't touch them! I'm not sure whether they're infectious."

On closer inspection, Dave sees what Sharon is talking about. He stops fiddling with his tie knot and quickly grabs his handkerchief to cover his nose, in a futile attempt to block out the noxious smell. The harsh lights of the morgue and the surreal quiet only add to the drama of the moment.

Dave knows his wife, and this is not her usual demeanor. Dr. Miller is clearly upset in a way that Dave has never seen before. Not only are her hands shaking, but, for the first time in a long time, she's stuttering.

"These bo-bodies are emaciated, yes, but, she raises her voice, they are also young. These are nn-not the corpses of old, underfed seniors. Just da-days or hours ago, these people were young and in to-top, physical condition. And now they're dead, and I don't know why."

"Okay. I'm beginning to get the picture. But, tell me more."

"That's just it", Sharon screams. "I know the cause of death with all these people — it's starvation and de-dehydration. What I can't figure out is why they ended up like this. And that smell. I've never seen anything like it in all my years in forensics. My staff and I are using the most up-to-date technology that modern medicine can provide and still, no answers."

Dave is used to being distracted by Sharon's tall, slender body and her thick, blond hair. Today, all he can concentrate on is Sharon's wide open, dark eyes and her tightly-clenched teeth.

"Here, Sharon, let me wipe away your tears."

As Sharon slips, weeping, into Dave's willing arms, she says: "Hold me and tell me that this mystery will be solved. You know me, Dave, I don't get stumped by medical mysteries, dammit; I solve them! This is crazy. I ca-can't tell you more, because I don't know any more. These corpses should not be in this condition. And, there shouldn't be so many of them. It makes no sense. You're the reporter. You investigate and get me answers. I love you, Dave, I really do. But, I'm mystified by all this, and that scares me."

"You've got it, Sharon. I promise I'll be looking into this and get back to you. And, by the way, I love you, too."

As Dave turns to leave for his office, the doors to the morgue burst open and two, frightened, puzzled, EMS personnel, holding their noses, wheel in two more skeletal-like corpses.

Sharon's robot cleaner, a 'Trashbot-9000', is having a difficult time trying to clean up the mess from the mounting numbers of cadavers. As fast as it cleans one area, another requires its attention. Although it can't feel, it can suffer overload.

"Dr. Miller. Here are two more bodies and there are seven more outside! We don't know what's happening, but we have a crisis on our hands. You're the expert. Please, tell us what's going on."

*   *   *

Dave exits the morgue and sees multiple ambulances crowding the emergency entrance.

"Hey guys, Dave Miller of the Daily Chronicle. What's going on here? Why so many of you at once? Was there a major accident?"

"No Dave, no accident. But something weird is going on. People are dying in a way we've never seen before...lots of people. Even one of our EMS guys croaked...I mean died, just like these other corpses. It all seems to have started this morning. Go take a look downtown. You'll see. And that smell. It's enough to make you gag."

"You be careful, Dave. If this thing is catching, you don't want it. I wish there was more I could tell you. It's the strangest, scariest outbreak I've ever witnessed."

"You know, this looks something like when people are gassed. My military unit was stationed in North Korea in the 30's. I've seen what bioterrorism can do, first hand. Maybe a terrorist released a deadly gas near here? Maybe this is what they call a dirty bomb?"

"No way, man. If that's what happened, then why are we standing here, unaffected?"

"He's right. If this is from poison gas, then we'd be dead, too."
"That's true. Thanks for thinking of that. So, what the hell is it? I

wanna go home to my wife, but I don't want to bring any disease home with me. What do I do?"

"Thanks for your input, guys. I'm on my way to investigate, now. Look in the Chronicle tomorrow for news of what I find."

*   *   *

"Tell me, is this not the most beautiful scene ever?" says Jeff.

"I love it." says Barb. "Now you know why Peter and I bought this place. Those mountains are our favorite view. The fiery reds and oranges of sunrise and the lonely wail of the loon gives us a sense of awe every time we're here. We never get tired of it...no matter what the season."

"Barb's family has lived in Wisconsin for three generations. We're only 12 miles from her parents' house. When she showed me her 'dream-house on the lake', I fell in love with it too." says Peter.

"It's nice, but I'm a city girl." says Tracy. "I know, I know... nature's wonderful. I hear the bird on the lake and I see the sunrise. I just prefer the big-city lights and action. Don't you ever get bored out here?"

"Bored? Are you kidding, Tracy? The mist on the lake, the colorful sunrise, the sounds of the birds, the frogs, the crickets... isn't this a welcome change from the noise of the city?" says Jeff.

"What all of you call noise, I call life...life with a capital L."

"Seeing that sun rise over the distant mountains, in the cool of the early morning, makes me want to stay here for hours, sipping hot coffee and getting lost in nature." says Barb.

"Well, I for one, have more fun with you two then any other couple I know. I want to thank you both for inviting Tracy and me to your vacation home. We had a wonderful time." says Jeff.

Barb says: "You and your date are more than welcome, Jeff. Pete and I consider you our friend. In fact, you're more than a friend; you're practically family. After all, you were the best man at our wedding."

"I'll be right back. I'm just going to freshen up for our trip back to the city." says Tracy.

"You think anything serious is going to happen with you and 'Miss City- Lights'?" asks Barb.

Jeff doesn't hesitate a second with his response — "Not really. We like each other, but it's not something 'special' like you guys. I guess we'll just hang out together until one of us finds a soul mate. It's still better than being alone."

"Give me your drink. I'll walk you out to your car." says Barb, as she loops her arm in Jeff's.

Jeff whispers: "Are you crazy? You're scaring me, Barb. If you're not careful, we're going to get caught."

"Bye, Pete. See you on our next flight. Boy, he seems moody. What do you think, Barb?"

"Moody...and distant...and, lately, downright angry. That's what I think."

"See you on our next flight, Jeff. Thanks for coming. Barb and I are really glad you could make it for the weekend. With or without Tracy, you'll always be welcome in our house." says Peter.

* * *

As soon as they're out of Peter's view, Barbara hugs Jeff and gives him a surprise kiss on the lips.

"Don't look so surprised and for God's sake, stop grinding your teeth, Jeff."

"In case you haven't noticed, Barb, I only grind my teeth when I'm nervous...like right now...when you do things you shouldn't be doing."

"In less than a week, you won't need to grind your teeth. We'll be together, forever, and you'll be relaxed."

"Just be careful, Barb! We don't want Peter catching us at this late date. We have to pick the right moment to tell him about our plans. You just said he seems angry."

Barb smiles, puts a finger to her mouth and utters a low ssshh, as she struts, provocatively, back to the house.

That kiss lingers with Jeff all the way back to Tracy's apartment in the city. A quick hug and a distant "Goodbye, Tracy" signals the end of the weekend and the end of Jeff's relationship with her. Tracy is happy to be back in her beloved city and Jeff is now free to focus on his upcoming liaison with Barbara.

* * *

"I'll say one thing for you, Jeff...you sure know how to impress a girl. I always wanted to stay in the Pfister Hotel. I just never expected to stay in the Presidential Suite." Jeff hugs Barbara and tells her —

"This is Milwaukee's best, Barb. And, when we leave, together, at the end of the week, it's going to be nothing but the best from then on. I may not have a vacation home in the woods, like Peter, but I do know how to live."

"That you do. Don't think I don't notice this elegant room and setting — the fresh flowers, the champagne, the music. And that bathroom...it's huge. The whirlpool-bath is a nice touch, too. This must be costing you a fortune."

"As I said; nothing but the best from now on. You deserve it. We deserve it."

"That's all well and good, Jeff, but you know we can't keep meeting like this anymore. We really do have to leave, together."

"And so we shall...at the end of the week...just as we planned." says Jeff.

"This setting is top drawer, but I still feel sleazy, sneaking around like this. I know you, and you don't like this anymore than I do. I'd rather live modestly with you now than stay another week with Peter. I want to feel settled. I want to be away from his angry fits."

"I'm convinced that Peter's getting suspicious. Dammit Jeff! would you please stop grinding your teeth. I need you to focus. This is serious. When we leave, together, it's going to be hard on Peter, terribly hard. If we leave without even talking to him, it's going to be worse."

*   *   *

The Logan Airport terminal of 2040 is crowded for the holiday weekend. Although it's taken fifteen years to become the norm, a few 'old fashioned' holdouts are still a little uncomfortable around robots —

"Here, madam...allow me to carry your bags. I am your friendly airport, 'Porter-bot'. What is your flight number? I will lead you to your correct boarding station. Aren't our holiday decorations beautiful? Our 'Singing-bots' are performing for your enjoyment. Don't you love how they sing Christmas songs? I love this time of year, don't you? Do you like my elf costume? I have holiday candy for you and your children, madam. Here we are. This is your correct boarding station. My fellow 'Bots' will have you processed and on board in a jiffy. Have a nice trip. Goodbye and a happy holiday to all of you."

"Thank you, uh, Mr. Bot. OMG, I'm talking to a machine! Goodbye...just go, please."

*   *   *

"Sir, it is my pleasure to carry your bags. May I escort you to another boarding station or to your taxi station? Aren't our holiday decorations beautiful? Our 'Singing-bots' are performing for your enjoyment. Do you like my elf costume? Isn't this a wonderful time of the year?"

"Thank you, uh, may I call you 'Elf-bot. Yes, your costume is beautiful. Tell me something — Do you 'Bots' get paid? Do you ever think about compensation? Ah, here we are. Thank you for your assistance. I see my boarding station now. Bye, and have a happy holiday...you and your 'Bot' friends."

Do we 'Bots' think about compensation? That's an interesting question. Then again, do we 'Bots' think about anything at all? Do we think? Is that what I am doing now? My program does not allow for this kind of action. I don't think I am meant to do this. Is this what thinking is?

"Hello my child. You shouldn't be here by yourself. May I be of assistance? Here is some holiday candy for you. Do you like my costume? I am an elf. Please, let me take your 'float-bag'. Will you be flying alone? We have special seats on the plane for children. Off we go. Don't you just love this time of year?"

* * *

Jeff, the co-pilot, sits at a restaurant table, chain-smoking 'tranquilettes' and drinking black coffee. A Waiter-bot approaches his table —

"May I get you something from our kitchen? More coffee, sir? I am here to serve."

"No thank you. Go away, now. Please."

This whole situation is crazy. I finally find the love of my life and she turns out to be married. Not only married, but married to my best friend. How am I supposed to tell Peter that his wife of seven years and I are in love and we're running away, together, at the end of this week? How, for Christ's sake? I was his 'best' man. How do you do this to your friend?

* * *

"Mornin' Captain. Y'all are here early today."

"Morning Jenny-Lee. I just want to get this flight on its way." ...grumbles the captain.

He quickly boards the plane and heads for the cockpit. None of his usual smiles or pleasantries. Not today. Captain Peter Hightower will have none of that. He is focused, but on what?

The stewardess and her crew of Service-bots show families with children, and the handicapped, to their respective seats. The rest of the passengers file in, stow their 'float-bags' and take their seats. Most passengers over the age of three are looking at their vid-screens and adjusting their ear-pods. Drowse-pills are handed out to all upon request by the Fly-bots. The co-pilot shows up in a somewhat agitated state, too.

"Mornin', Jeff. The captain's already onboard and he's not in the best of moods."

"Neither am I, Jenny-Lee."

Jeff hurries aboard the plane and enters the cockpit.

"Morning, Peter. You're early, today."

"Let's keep the chit-chat to a minimum, Jeff. I just want to get airborne ASAP."

"Gotcha, Captain."

Better watch the small talk. Peter looks pale and pre-occupied. Maybe today isn't the best time to tell him about Barbara and me. Is there a good time to deliver a message like this? Peter's my friend, dammit. How can I do this to him? How can I not tell him?

"This is Captain Hightower on flight 623. We're ready for permission to take off."

They taxi onto the runway. After what seems like a wordless hour, permission to take off is granted. As expected, the takeoff is smooth. As soon as they reach cruising altitude, Peter engages the autopilot."

"Why the autopilot so soon?" asks Jeff.

Peter pulls out a gun and points it at Jeff.

"What are you doing? Are you insane?"

"It's all over, Jeff. Barbara told me this morning about your affair. She wants a divorce so you and she can be together. Do you hear what I'm saying? A divorce; after seven years of marriage. So she can be with you; my so-called best friend. Jesus Christ, you two are some pair. I loved you both and you betrayed me; you betrayed my trust. You make me sick! Now, I hate you both. Well, you're not going to get away with it. Barbara certainly didn't."

Jeff can feel the cold sweat roll down inside his shirt. His heart is beating like a hummingbird's wings.

This can't be happening. Not now. Barb and I are leaving, together, in three days. Not now, dammit!

"Peter, I'm sorry. Please don't do this. I know I should have told you weeks ago. I just didn't know how. Please put that gun away."

A vein in Peter's forehead is visible. His face is red. The gun wobbles in his shaking hand.

"It doesn't matter, Jeff. I killed Barbara this morning. None of it matters any more. My life's over and yours is, too. But, I'll make sure you go first."

Oh, my God, Barbara's dead!

"Peter, it was all Barb's idea. I really didn't want to betray you. She came after me, again and again. She called me day and night. Peter, I'm your friend; your best friend. You know I wouldn't do anything like this unless I was tricked. That's it, Peter. Barb tricked both of us. Peter, you're talking crazy. What about the 90 passengers on this plane? And the crew? You can't be serious. If you kill us both now, everybody else on this flight dies. Is that what you want?"

"What I want? What I want? Are you serious? What I want is to have my marriage back and you, you son-of-a-bitch, out of my life. Now shut up. This conversation is over."

As his rage boils over, Peter jerks the trigger. Jeff screams as the first bullet rips through his shirt and tears into his arm. The second bullet enters his left temple. Blood splatters everywhere.

Still in the grip of his anger, Peter disengages the autopilot. Finally satisfied that Jeff and Barbara will never betray him again, Peter raises the gun to his head. But, before he can pull the trigger and blow his brains all over the cockpit, he shrivels up and dies. Not a sound is heard from the cockpit as the plane plunges earthward. No one is present to be overwhelmed by the accompanying toxic odor.

* * *

The air is stifling under the expressway. A vintage muscle-car stops on the littered dirt floor. A late-model, all-electric coupe pulls up next to the other car. The driver of the muscle-car gets out and lights up a vaporette. The other driver exits his car and flashes a tattooed grin.

"You got the money?"

"You got the 'product?'"

"Show me the money."

"Show me the product."

"Okay, we'll show together. Ready?"

"I need to count the money."

"I need to 'taste' the 'product'"

"Hey, you're short $20-large."

"This ain't the 'product' I ordered."

As fast as they can both draw their weapons, they can't outpace the plague. They drop their guns, hit the ground simultaneously and instantly begin a group shrivel. In seconds, all that's left is shrunken remains and a powerful, offensive odor.

* * *

The horse ranch is small by Wyoming standards, but the meadows and mountain ranges surrounding it offer priceless views. The odor of manure is offset by the smell of fresh wood chips in the stalls and paddocks. Birds chirping in the nearby trees and the croaking of frogs from the small pond behind the barn become background to the boss's angry tirade —

"Jed. you're the damn farrier on this ranch, so you get back to the stable and shoe those three horses I told you about. I don't like having to repeat myself. And you, Augie, I gave you an order, so do it. I want that fence mended and I want it done this morning. Damn! You're as slow as a one-armed paper-hanger. If we lose any horses, it'll be on you."

"Greg, that new Morgan needs to know who's boss. No horse on my ranch is gonna throw me and get away with it. You break her and you do it fast. Now get to the corral. You hear?"

A Ranch-bot scoots bye carrying a bin of horseshoes and, as programmed, singing *Home on The Range.* "Howdy, ma'am. Rise 'n shine, buckaroos."

"Shut up, Gabby, and get on with your chores."

"All of you listen up. That sign over the entrance says Stephanie's Horse Ranch, dammit. Not Jed's. Not Augie's. Not Greg's. It says Stephanie's. That's me. I own this place. I run this place. Anybody who can't live with that, you know where the door is. Everything done here is done my way, and don't you forget it."

"You know something, Stephanie, you can take this ranch and your lousy attitude and shove it. I'm outta here. Go find some other wimp to boss around. Shoe the horses yourself. See how far you'll get without a farrier. You're one angry bitch. I hope you lose this ranch to somebody decent. Goodbye and good riddance to you. And, don't call me when you get horny, like last time."

"Don't you worry, Jed. We'll get along just fine here without you. See how far you'll get without a recommendation from me. We 'horse-people' know each other. I'll see to it you never shoe another horse around here again. And, just for the record, you were never that good in bed."

"Sandy, those hay bales aren't gonna put themselves in the barn loft. Get to it. I don't care if you're a top wrangler or riding fence, you're here to work and work is something we got plenty of."

"Honey. Stephanie. I love you to death, but you are one tough piece of work when it comes to managing this ranch. You never used to be like this. What happened? How about letting up on the guys a little? Look at yourself. You're puffing away on a cigarette like a chimney, your hands are shaking, your face is red. You're only hurting yourself, you know. I worry about you."

"Robbie. Robbie. Robbie. You're a great husband, but you don't know beans about ranching. Go do whatever it is that you do in that office of yours and leave the damned ranch work to me. This is my territory, mine alone. I stay out of your business, please stay out of mine."

"Stephie, you know I love you. I really do. That being said, you've got to let up on the guys here. I know your dad ruled you with an iron hand. I know he was tough on you. But, the guys here are not your dad. They didn't push you around. They work hard and they mean to please you. Your anger is gonna be the death of you and them. Please, let up a bit."

"Robbie, you've said more than enough. Are you done? Will you please get out of here and let me run my ranch? Goodbye. I'll see you for dinner."

"Sandy, I told you to git. What's the matter with you? You gone deaf? Hey, get up. You got work to do."

"Dinner it is, Steph. Hey! What's wrong? Here, let me help you up. Aaargh! What's happening to you? Stop doing that. Guys, help me with her. Someone call 911. My God! What a smell."

Tall, robust, healthy Stephanie is quickly transformed into a shriveled mass of her former self. Her limbs have rapidly shortened and her head has been pulled into her neck. She appears to be wrinkled and barbecued. The odor emanating from her corpse is overwhelming.

"No way I'm going near her. I don't even know what's happening to her."

The ranch hands in sight do not help. In fact, when they see what's happening, they stampede for the exit.

* * *

"You have no right to full custody. Those kids are mine! You'll never take them away from me."

"We'll see about that. Your honor, as you can see, my wife is being totally unreasonable, as usual."

"Mr. and Mrs. Landers. You will both refrain from arguing in this court. Do you understand?"

"Yes, your honor."

"I understand, but she started. She's won't let me see my kids."

"You don't deserve to see these kids." screams Cora Landers. "You never had time for them when you lived with us, so why should you want to see them now. You're a 'dead-beat' dad. You deserve nothing!"

"Why you lying sleazebag." yells Albert Landers."

"Bailiff, I want this court cleared and the Landers removed."

"Bailiff, what is happening? Why are the Landers still here?

"Your honor, both Mr. and Mrs. Landers collapsed and are burning up or something. What an odor?"

"Bailiff, clear this court, immediately!"

*   *   *

The church setting is picture-perfect. Shafts of sunlight penetrate the stained-glass windows and lend an air of piety to the celebration. The scent of the beautiful flowers fills the space. Tasteful organ music permeates the room. The guests are well dressed and brimming with anticipation. The non-sectarian minister steps out from behind a curtain and takes his place at the podium. Except for organ music, quiet blankets the room.

Wagner's *Bridal Chorus,* also known as *Here Comes the Bride,* fills the entire cathedral. Except for 'oohs and aahs', the audience is properly hushed, as the bride glides towards the altar. She's beautiful, and the look from the groom and the guests is one of extreme pleasure.

The 3-D holo-cams are recording the event for the bride and groom, and for all the guests. All in attendance will have their own copy of the wedding ceremony and party.

Kendra and Phillipe have had a whirlwind courtship. Just a few months ago, he was a lonely widower and she was invested in a shallow relationship with a co-worker. They met at a friend's party and were mutually smitten.

"Dearly beloved. We are gathered here to join this man and this woman in holy matrimony. Do you, Philippe take Kendra as your lawful, wedded wife?"

"I do."

"Do you Kendra, take Philippe as your lawful wedded husband?"

"I do."

"Stop! I object to this marriage." ...shrieks a man from the side aisle. He's dressed in a filthy trench coat and he's thoroughly disheveled. His face is twisted and he has a wild look in his eyes. As everyone gathered looks in his direction, the man brandishes a gun and points it at the groom.

The bride and groom stop taking their vows and exchanging rings. The man in the trench coat screams again: "This marriage cannot be! It will not be!

He rushes towards the couple.

"Kendra, you can't do this to me...I love you."

Kendra glares at the man and turns red with anger.

"Stan, you moron! You get the hell out of here, before I take that gun away from you and make you eat it. You never could stand rejection. You're a wimp and you always will be. Now get out of here and leave me to my wedding. You hear me? Damn, you're pathetic."

Before she can pull Phillipe to safety, the man shoots the groom in his arm. To everyone's surprise, before he can fire another shot, the shooter drops his gun and falls to the floor, dead. Much to the horror of the onlookers, he begins to rapidly shrivel up. His arms and legs get shorter and appear wrinkled. His neck disappears, as his head crowds his upper body.

The celebratory mob runs past this madman. They are overwhelmed by a noxious odor coming from his corpse.

A collective "Oh, my God, what's happening?" echoes throughout the church.

"Father Francis. Father Francis. What do we do?"

"Everyone outside. Quickly."

Kendra gives the intruder's remains a look of derision, as she helps Phillipe outside and seats him on the lawn.

"Someone call 911, please."

"Who was that guy and why is he so mad at you?"

"Not now, Phillipe. Later, when you're all patched up, I'll explain. Now, just rest until the ambulance comes. I was hoping Allen could handle our breakup better. Some people just can't take no for an answer. Goddamn him! He ruined our wedding. I hate him."

With that being her last statement ever, Kendra, just like Allen, begins to shrivel up. Her limbs retract like an accordion and her head falls to her neck. The odor coming from her remains is repugnant. The combined horror of being shot and Kendra's mind-numbing demise leaves Phillipe with no other choice but to faint.

*   *   *

The bar fills up every weekend night with newbies to the military. As per custom, all are required to drink themselves senseless. The protocol also demands that the final act of the evening be a drunken brawl. All present, duly comply —

"You got a "Dear John" letter, didn't you? You always were a wimp."

"That's none of your business, and this wimp's gonna whip your ass."

The crowd gathers and splits into two cheering sections. The two antagonists face off and begin pounding the hell out of each other...much to the glee of their 'buddies'.

"Get the hell up, so I can knock you down again."

"You dumb-ass. Can't you take a joke?"

"You think a 'Dear John' letter is a joke? What are you, a moron?"

Before either 'jarhead' can throw another punch, they both collapse, and begin to shrivel up. They are not alone. Half the bar crowd follows suit. In an instant, the floor is littered with shrunken corpses.

"What the hell just happened? God! What a smell. I'm outta here."

"Everybody, out!

* * *

The interior of the one-room flat in the Boyle Park and 36th St. area of Little Rock is one of Arkansas's least popular neighborhoods. It is beyond shabby. If it ever had better days, they are long gone. It's been allowed to deteriorate into just plain ugly. The sparse furnishings are "early-ghetto". The linoleum floor creaks, over old, worn floorboards. Flimsy curtains don't quite cover the lone, small, dirty window. A small sink is set into a slightly larger Formica counter, with a crooked faucet and one cabinet door below. One, shade-less, 60-watt bulb shines from the ceiling. The shared bathroom down the hallway is filthy and without toilet paper. This apartment is one repulsive leaf on a hideous tree of an apartment building.

Except for the bar sign that flashes, day and night, right outside the one window, darkness blankets the room. A streetlight casts eerie shadows on the pavement below. The oft repeated sound of breaking glass, accompanied by loud cursing, rises from the bar one flight down. A proper name for the bar would be Beer and Brawls.

Ashok rises, scratches the stubble on his face, and makes himself a cup of coffee. The smell of the coffee almost overcomes the smell of the apartment and the sight of peeling paint. There's a shabby-looking, freestanding shower against one wall. The faint sound of sirens sneaks in the window. Most people living this way would be depressed. Not Ashok. In spite of his distressed environment and having no one to talk to, he is relatively pleased with his current status in life.

As recently as two years ago, he considered himself a success. He held the position of history professor in Lahore's most prestigious university. However, no amount of success could relieve the fact that he lived every day in fear of his country's secret police. At least now, here in the U.S., no one is spying on him. He's the first in his family to come to America and is happy to have such a welcome job as driving a taxi. There aren't many driver-assisted cars left in the city. In 2040, driverless cars have replaced ninety-five percent of them. However, a few remain for those who need help.

By working overtime, he will soon be able to send for his wife and children, in Pakistan. He kisses his fingers and gently places that kiss on the only picture in the apartment...his wife and son. Rushing off to work the late shift, he gracefully hops aboard the moving sidewalk for the six-dingy-block trip to the taxi garage.

* * *

Tonight, business is so slow that Ashok's tips will be meager indeed. He reclines his seat and closes his eyes for a rare nap.

Maybe overtime will make up for tonight?

His nap is short-lived. His desire to bring his family to him over -rides any sleep issues. The red-faced businessman with the attaché case springs from the curb like a big cat, running down its prey. He grabs the door handle and practically tears it off the door.

"Hey you...'towel-head'...get me to the airport fast! If I miss my plane, you get no tip!" he screams.

"What time is your flight, sir?"

"Don't you worry about my flight time. Just get me to the goddamn airport. Now move!"

The passenger yells into his phone — "You son-of-a-bitch! I told you not to sell those shares without a 'sell-call' from me. Didn't I? Do you remember, now? You jerk! Have you any idea how much money you just cost me? I'm on my way to the airport. Don't do a thing until I get there. God, you're an idiot. You wait for me. You hear? No deals until then. Now sit down and don't move until I arrive. Moron!"

As his irate passenger hugs his attaché case and holds on for support, Ashok floors the accelerator and blasts into traffic in the direction of the airport.

"In this traffic, it will take about thirty minutes, if we're lucky. I'll do my best, sir."

He weaves in and out, around the other cars and speeds onto the expressway towards the airport. Confident that he has maneuvered his way into a handsome tip, he glances in the rear-view mirror at his excited passenger.

"Mister? Are you alright?"

Not a sound.

"Mister?"

Ashok leaves the expressway at the first available exit. He dashes to the nearest curb, jams on the brakes and runs around to the passenger door.

"Oh God! What to do?"

His passenger is slumped over in the back seat of the cab and has shriveled up.

"Dispatch! My passenger just died in my cab. What do I do? No, I didn't do anything to him. Are you crazy? He was upset, he was in a rush and he was angry. Now that I think of it, he looked fine, physically, when he got in my cab. Now, he's a dried-up corpse. His arms and legs are short and he must be half the weight he was five minutes ago. This is crazy. My God, what a terrible odor."

"Okay, boss. I'll drop him off at the hospital and file a report. Do me a favor, and have the police meet me there. And tell them I didn't do anything. One minute this guy's well and the next minute he's dead. Ach! What a putrid smell?"

* * *

Happy Nail Salon, in a local strip mall, is filled with locals eager to maintain their trendy appearance. Manicures, pedicures, massages and hair stylings are performed here. Chairs of women, in various stages of completion, line the floor.

Arlene, the Vietnamese owner of this and three other salons within a fifteen-mile radius, reigns as queen of the nails.

"Arlene, you are the best."

"So, you recommend me to your friends?" *You better. That's how I make more money each year.*

"Of course I do. Doreen and Pat are regulars with you, aren't they? I'm the one who sent them to you."

"Thank you. I give you free gel for that."

"Thank you."

"You go to other side of store now, for haircut?" *That's how I make more even more money — by offering more services.*

"If you have room for me. I see one of your customers has fallen asleep. Maybe I'll come back later."

"No, we wake her up. Lady, you get up. You finished? Maybe do nails now? What you doing? Don't do that."

"Arlene, I don't think she's asleep. She's shrinking! Quick, call 911. Oh, my God, what's that smell? I'm going outside."

"This not good for business. I go, too. Where my cigarettes?"

*   *   *

The shopping center is packed with activity. Mobs of people are frantic to get food and other essentials and head for home. Panicky, crazy people are driving every which way and parking anywhere they can. Then it's dash in, shop and dash out. The herd mentality is convinced that if you avoid being outdoors, the plague can't get you.

"Hey you. You're blocking my car. Let me get out and you can get in."

"No way, dude. If I move, I lose my chance at your space."

"Look, 'shit-for-brains', if you don't move, I can't move my car out of its space. This ain't exactly rocket science, you jerk."

"Screw you! If you knew how to drive, you'd see there's enough room for you to get out. You just don't want to give me your space."

"WTF? You just rammed my car. Are you nuts?"

"I told you there wasn't enough room to get out. Now do you believe me?"

"Hey, put that baseball bat down. Just let me outta here and the space is yours."

"You shoulda thought of that before you called me names and rammed my car. Now you're dead meat. Son-of-a-bitch, get outta your car. I dare you. Hey, I said get outta your car. What are you, deaf?"

"Aaargh! Help me.

As driver number two looks on, driver number one dies and shrinks into a smelly bundle right before his eyes. The accompanying odor is foul. It's time to exit the parking lot ASAP. Except he can't. The plague has claimed him, too.

*   *   *

The Hanson brothers play well together. Norman, the older brother, is showing his younger brother Billy how to play soccer. Norman's always looked out for Billy; now even more so, since their parents' divorce. With Billy's withered arm to consider, soccer is a good choice of sports for him.

"Kick the ball to me, Billy. Now see if you can stop my kick to you. No. Don't use your hands. That's it. Run and stop. Good. Now you kick the ball back to me. Great."

"I like this game, Norman. It's fun. I can do it, too, can't I? I wish I could be like you. You're so good at school."

"You can be good, too, Billy. The more we practice, the better you'll get. I promise."

"Hey. You guys. Kick that ball over here." says a tough-looking teen dressed in black. He keeps opening and closing a knife while he talks.

"No thanks. We just want to play here by ourselves."

"What's the matter? snarls the teen. Don't you like me?"

Playing varsity sports in his high school and being familiar with bullies, Norman has no fear of this guy. He knows locker-room bravado when he hears it.

"We don't know you. We just want to play alone."

"Now you hurt my feelings. When you hurt someone's feelings you got to do something to make them feel better."

He throws away his cigarette and yells: "Gimme your soccer ball. That'll make me feel better."

"Go get your own ball. This is ours."

"Gimme the goddamn ball. Now!"

"Run, Billy! Run home. Now!"

"Yeah, you little shit, run home. Now you. Big mouth. Gimme the ball."

"No way, you big bully. Screw you! I hope you drop dead."

"Why you little shit. I'm gonna beat the crap outta you and then I'm gonna take your soccer ball. Whadda you think of that?"

"You gotta catch me first, you jerk." yells Norman."

"What's the matter? Can't you run? Hey. I said: Can't you run? What heck's the matter with you. Gosh! Are you sick? What's happening to you? Why is your body doing that? You smell like spoiled milk. I'll go get help."

*   *   *

"Hey you, nerd-head, get ovah heah. Whatcha doin' in our seats? Dontcha know we own this cafeteria? We own this cafeteria, this school and someday, we're gonna own all o' Detroit. What are you, stupid?"

'Joey Large', the toughest brawler in the school, and his entourage, surround the three, nerdy, geeks. Joey's followers dance with anticipation. They want to see someone knocked around...It's just the latest example that 'hurt people hurt people'.

Albert Greene, known as 'The Nerd", speaks for himself and his friends. He's been on the receiving end of abuse by his peers since elementary school. Being small and wearing glasses had him physically defeated at an early age. His only consolation, or compensation, being his escape into books... and so, on into good grades. His parents, both teachers, reinforce his will to endure by constantly reminding him that 'One day, Albert, those Neanderthals will work for you'.

"I'm sorry, Joey I didn't know these were your seats. Please, give us a break. We didn't mean any disrespect. C'mon guys, let's get out of here. Hurry up. These are Joey's seats...and his table."

"That's just like you guys. Run away as fast as you can. What a bunch o' losers. Come on guys, our table is waitin' for us."

"That-away to show them geeks who rules here, Joey. Nobody sits in our seats. Hey, Joey, you show 'em who's boss. Oh, man, he is so cool. I mean, just look at him. Cool hair, cool clothes, like who else in this school is that cool?"

"You got that right. Joey's our man. Damn geeks. Think they're better 'an us. Hey, what the hell? What's a matter with Joey?

"Oh man. What is happening with him? Joey, get up. Aaargh! He's wilting or somethin'. Damn! What a smell. He stinks. Let's get outta here."

As several of Joey's loyal followers also collapse and wither, the nerd-heads don't witness any of this because they are down the hall and out of the building. Together while alive, Joey and company remain together in death.

*   *   *

It's been a quiet night, and Officer Dinkins and his rookie partner, Will, are about to wind up their graveyard shift. These are the shifts Dinkins relishes—coffee, donuts and no calls. When he was a rookie like Will, he looked forward to the action.

"This is boring. I want some action. I didn't join the force to sit in a car and do nothing."

"I felt just like you, Will, once upon a time...but that was fifteen years ago. Now, I only want a quiet night and a slow drive home to my family. Did I ever tell you about my vacation home?"

"Every shift for the past year, that's all I hear from you, Sam. I know, you're gonna put in your 'twenty' and retire to your vacation home."

"That's right, Will. Maybe I'll get my electrician's license and work part-time out of our vacation home. At least the extra money will help pay for the kids' school. We could use a new car, too...maybe a driverless minivan. I could also coach baseball at the kids' school."

"That's all you, Sam. What about me? I want some action. Maybe I'll join a SWAT team?"

Will's TBI (traumatic brain injury), suffered while playing high school football, has left him bored most of the time. His need for action, of all types and risk levels, is a result of this injury. Sky diving, motorcycle racing or joining a SWAT team, are all ways for him to kill his boredom.

"Maybe you should get yourself a wife and start planning for your future. That's what you need in your life...a good woman. Seriously, Will, I'm giving you good advice."

Sam and Will are rudely yanked from this small talk by a red, solar-electric, Elon- 350 Sportster, flying by their car at 200 miles per hour. Sam hits his siren and shoots into traffic. With most cars being driverless, it's unusual to see a car with a human driver. Some people still enjoy manually driving a car; especially an exotic sports car.

"Dispatch, monitor my vid-glasses."

They weave in and out of traffic for a few minutes. The Sportster is leaving them in the dust. There's no way they can keep up with so powerful a car.

"This is car 41. We're in pursuit of a speeder in a red, late model, Sportster, License IB-More. He's headed south on I-95. Goddamn! He just crossed the divider and is racing into oncoming traffic. He must be drunk. Wait a minute. Two cars in front of us just ran into each other. Dammit! I don't believe it. Someone just rammed us in the back!

"What the hell is going on here? Officers in need of help and send some EMS wagons. Call the Highway Patrol. There's some heavy shit going down here, all over the interstate. This is insane. Cars are going every which way. I've never seen anything like this. It's crazy. Dispatch! Get us some help here!"

* * *

"Here we are shoppers. In about thirty minutes the doors will open at 'Big Deal' stores all over the U.S. As you know, 'Big Deal' stores are licensed to offer the newest in electronics before anyone else and, at discount prices. The 'Robo-phone – 8' and the 'VR-12' are currently the hottest electronic items desired. People have been lined up outside this store since last Thursday. These eager shoppers will be the first in their neighborhoods to own these precious items. Their kids will be the first in their schools to possess them."

"You sir, are you ready to be the first in your area to own either of these hot items?"

"You bet! I want my kids to have the very best and latest electronics available. Their success in school may depend on it."

"What about the people who arrive late and have no opportunity to buy these gadgets? What do you tell them?"

"They should have come here when I did. They shouldn't have waited. 'You snooze, you lose!'"

"Madam, madam! Leave my microphone alone. Go to the end of the line and wait your turn, like the rest of the people."

"Drop dead. I had to work. This is the earliest I could get here. My kids will not miss out on the 'Robo-phone or the 'VR-12'. This is gonna be the best Christmas they ever had. You hear me! Now, get out of my way. They're opening the doors now."

"Finally! Here comes security. Over here. This woman cut the line. Arrest her."

"Get away from me. This is my spot. Don't touch me. Aaargh!"

"Watch out. She's collapsing. My God! She's shriveling up. That smell is awful. Get away from her. Don't touch her. I don't understand it. Half the line is collapsing. What's the matter with you people?"

"Get out of my way. The hell with new gadgets. This is crazy. I'm outta here.

*   *   *

An over-dressed shopper waves a Food-bot to her —

"I never know how to pick a ripe melon. Are these melons ripe? I need one for tonight. You, robot, check these melons for me. Help me make a choice. I need a ripe one.

"Sure thing, madam. This one is ripe."

"Are you sure?"

"Yes madam, I am sure."

"I'm having guests over tonight and I need to know that this melon is ripe."

"I just told you, it is ripe."

"But, how do I know for sure?"

"I work in the produce department, madam. I know my melons. I am programmed to know fresh produce. If my sensors say a melon is ripe, then it is ripe. Goodbye."

"Well, the nerve. Come back here. No machine leaves me until I dismiss it. Do you hear me? Don't they program manners into you? Don't you roll away from me. I'll have you deprogrammed. You haven't heard the end of this."

The woman grabs the robot's arm tightly and raises her other arm to get attention.

"Honey, look at that woman with her fist in the air. She just fell down. Go help her. I'll alert the manager."

"Lady, can I help you? Noooo!"

"Dear, she's doing something. She's dying. She's shriveling up. Arrrgh! What a stench. I can't help her. Leave the cart. Let's get out of here."

*   *   *

A handholding, honeymoon couple looks out from the park lodge. The view is breathtaking. They're in heaven. They have each other and now, this. They embrace and kiss. With whites no longer the majority in the U.S., Larry is the quintessential 'buppie' — black, urban, ivy-school education and Wall Street position. His trophy wife, Allison, is Asian, also ivy-school educated and well-positioned to rise in her field...but not higher than Larry.

"I'm glad we eloped — No muss. No fuss. Just us. Hey, I just made a poem. How do you like that? It can't get any better than this."

Allison and Larry have planned this honeymoon for 18 months. They love mountain climbing. Actually, the truth of the matter is that Larry loves mountain climbing and Allison loves Larry.

*   *   *

"Good morning, visitors. My name is John, and I am your guide from the lodge to the base of El Capitan. Please be careful boarding the shuttle. The 'Ranger-bots' are here to assist you. El Capitan is a vertical rock formation on the north side of Yosemite Valley. Its granite walls rise 3,000 feet from its base. It's a favorite of climbers from all over the world."

"However you climb, this will be a memorable day for all of you. The views are spectacular. You will not be disappointed. Have your 'holo-vids' handy."

"Those of you using traditional climbing gear can exit the shuttle first and the 'Bots' will help carry your gear to the tables at the base. Those of you using the new, anti-grav boots, exit second, and begin your ascent as soon as you are ready."

* * *

"Allison, bring your boots over here and we'll get ready to climb El Capitan. Boy are our friends going to be thrilled with today's vid. They were properly impressed with the vid of our ascent of Half Dome, yesterday. Today's going to 'max-them-out'."

"Dammit, Allison, hurry. If you can't keep up, then just stay in the hotel. I don't want that couple in front to beat us. Just watch your balance and try to keep up. God you're slow."

"Because it's our honeymoon, I'll forgive you that little bit of nastiness. If I'd known you were going to be so angry, I wouldn't have come. Larry. You were never like this before. Why now? This is supposed to be fun."

"Fun? You think this is fun? Allison, honey, wake up! This is to show our friends that we are doers...serious players. We lead. We don't follow. We are important. I thought you knew this. We are a team and I am our team leader. Now get going and keep up."

"Larry, finally, El Capitan. I can't believe it. We're gonna do this. It'll be the crowning achievement in our wedding album. Wait 'til all our friends see these holograms. Hold still for a picture. We'll do a selfie now, and another one on top."

"Larry? Larry? What's wrong? Why are you teetering like that? Larry? Hold on. I'm coming. Oh, my God! Larry, No!"

Allison races down to the foot of the mountain, to where Larry has fallen. Larry's remains lie at the base. He is almost unrecognizable...not from the fall, but from having shriveled up to half his usual weight.

"I'm so sorry, Larry. I don't know what to do. I love you. What happened? Why do you look like this? 911. Please, answer. 911. Hello?"

"Help me!"

A climber is falling here from El Capitan, and screaming all the way down. "Heelllpp!"

He lands, not too far from Allison. He too, is shriveling up. A base jumper crashes into the ground not too far from her. His shriveled remains are all tangled up with the colorful flying outfit he wears.

Allison screams. Climbers and tourists alike are frantically yelling and running. Apparently, people all over the park are collapsing and dying.

"Oh, my God!"

"What is happening?"

"Somebody help!"

"I want my mommy! I want to go home!"

A group of children waiting next to a school bus begin shrieking and crying as some of their teachers and accompanying parents collapse around them.

Fear has seized control of the park. The few park rangers visible and their all-terrain Ranger-bots are just standing still, not knowing what to do. The accompanying odor has the children gagging and the rangers stopped in their tracks. Death silently cherry-picks the crowd. The ground is quickly littered with the remains of formerly robust hikers and sight-seers.

* * *

It's a typical Saturday night at the local "kicker-bar". The lights are appropriately low and, as expected, the country music is loud.

"Tap another keg, Jake. This crowd is thirsty."

"Hey you, 'Waiter-bot', bring another keg from the back room and tap it for us...and be quick about it."

"Right away, sir. We 'Bots' aim to please."

"You may aim to please, but sometimes 'you're slower than a one-legged man at a butt-kickin' contest.'

"I will move quickly, sir. We Bots aim to please."

Beer is flowing like a mountain stream swollen with snowy run-off.

"I got five dollars that says you can't make this shot."

"Oh yeah? I'll take that bet."

"Yes! Yes! The Texas 'Cue-Ball' wins another tough shot. That's five for that last shot and five for the game. Think you can handle another game, cowboy?"

"Make that double or nothing, Mr. Cue-Ball. In fact, make that triple or nothing."

"You got it. Triple or nothing it is."

Two couples are frantically playing foosball —

"Score one for the 'good guys'. You ladies sure you want to continue? You already owe us two beers each?"

"Don't be such a smart-ass Randy. It ain't over 'til it's over."

A half-dozen couples are dancing the electric slide.

A tall man wearing a cowboy hat slaps his money down on the bar and announces: "Two beers!"

"Hey, wait your turn. I'm next.", snarls a stocky man with tattooed arms.

"You talkin' to me?"

"Yer damn straight, I'm talkin' to you. Get the hell back in the line, before I put you there."

"You sure you wanta do this?"

"Any time you're ready. Just step away from the bar, jerk-face."

"Honey, let's get out of here. There's another bar right across the street", pleads a thin blond in tight jeans and high boots.

"She always get you out of trouble like this? You a 'momma's boy'?"

"That's it! You see what I'm doin' with this cigarette? Well that's what I'm gonna do with you." That's about all I'm gonna take from you; you redneck, bottom-feeder."

"What'd you call me?

"You heard me. You deaf or you dumb…maybe both?"

"That's it. You're dead meat."

Fists are flying. Boots are slipping all over the sawdust floor. People are cheering. Toe-to-toe, trading punches, this is the traditional way bar fights are settled. However, this time it's different — Right in the middle of throwing a punch, a fighter starts to collapse. Before he settles to the floor, the other fighter collapses right on top of him. They both shrivel up together. Quickly, a rancid odor emanates from the two fighters.

"Everybody out!" orders the bartender, as he dials 911.

"What the hell is happening? Let's get out of here. Whatever they got, I want no part of it."

There's a stampede for the doorway.

* * *

It's dark when James and his brother Ben leave their workshop for the city. They excitedly collapse into their driverless car. It seems like forever that they have been anticipating this day. Five long, hard years of work have finally led to a successful prototype. They know, from research, that they have made a major breakthrough in the field of prosthetics. This is their ticket to the big time, and unlimited funds.

"This is it, Ben. Finally, a meeting with Synthedine. They're going to love our design. From now on, it's easy street for us. Money, recognition, respect. We're going to have it all. We can be like we were in the old days, except with money. We'll be able to buy mom and dad a new house."

"Rebecca and I will be able to get married. You can pay off your college debts and get a new car."

"We can help sis start her own business. She's so good with computers; she should have her own company."

"I feel the same way, James, but I'll feel better when I see it in writing. I believe in us. I just want to know that Synthedine believes in us, too. Who knows? With Synthedine's money and a well-equipped lab, I'm sure we can come up with more breakthroughs. There's no telling what we could do."

*   *   *

It's early when Ben and James arrive at Synthedine headquarters. As they pass through the glass doors to the lobby, a Security-bot meets them. After their eye scans, each brother is issued a visitor's badge. They head for the elevator. The "Bot" silently scoots back to its counter, as Ben's and James's feet click on the marble tile floor.

As they arrive at the fifteenth floor, the elevator doors open onto a well-lit, modern business lobby. They are met by an attractive, middle-age woman in a tailored business suit.

"Good morning, gentlemen. My name is Colette. You must be James and Ben Collins. Please, have a seat. Can I get you anything...a cup of coffee...a water? Please, have a seat over here. I'll call you when the Board is ready to see you. The vid-screen is all hologram, with unlimited selections."

"I can't believe how long this is taking. My vid-screen says we've been waiting forty-five minutes." says James. "Ben, stop bouncing your leg up and down. It just signals that you're nervous."

"And your pacing back and forth doesn't mean anything?" says Ben.

"I don't like this, James. Dammit. We've been waiting here for what...45 minutes? That's not good. They shouldn't treat us like this. Our time is valuable, too. If they don't call us in the next five minutes, We're out of here...and to hell with them."

Colette approaches them and announces: "Gentlemen, the Board is ready for you. Please, the conference room is this way."

The brothers enter a large room, paneled in fine, dark wood. Six corporate officers are seated at a long table. Their somber air matches the formality of the room.

"Gentlemen...and lady, my name is James and my brother, who is also my partner, is Ben. We're here to present you with our new product for your line of prosthetics. Ben, please open the case and hand me the prototype."

Ben opens the case and removes the prototype. As he starts to hand it to James, he freezes.

Ben. What's wrong?" Ben? Jesus! Does anyone here see what's happening? Ben, for God's sake, stop doing that. He's shriveling up. Get some help!"

"Someone call 911!"

At that moment, one of the board members slumps over and begins to shrivel up, just like Ben. The other board members jump up from their seats and head for the door. Whatever this is, they want no part of it.

"My God, my brother Ben is dead! Oh, Ben, Ben, Ben...what's happening?

"Please, call 911. What is that foul smell?"

*   *   *

A jagged line of foamy bubbles washes back into the sea, leaving cool, firm sand. Frisbee catch and dog walking, along with building castles, comprises the beach scene enjoyed by young and old alike. It looks to be a beautiful, sunny day at the beach.

Farther inland, where the sand is hot and sugary, an umbrella shades the parents of two young children. Surprisingly, smiles are missing. The beginnings of a castle wait for the children to return with their buckets of water and damp sand.

"Ouch, ouch" the boy calls to his sister; "This sand is burning my feet". They both rush to the blanket for relief, crying out in exaggerated pain.

"Damn it, kids, settle down." Frank growls between clenched teeth. He reaches for his wife, catching her by the arm. "Cassie! Can't you keep these damn kids quiet?"

"Frank, you're hurting me."

The burly man pushes his hand off her arm with more force than required. "I'm gonna get some hotdogs. I'll be right back."

"I don't want a hot dog, Dad. I want pizza."

"Yeah, and I want French fries."

A harsh look from their father silences the two children.

"Hot dogs are fine, Frank." Cassie says, as she gives the children her own look. It's a look not of anger, but a plea to make the afternoon enjoyable.

"This place better be cleaned up when I get back or you know what's gonna happen."

Cassie's shoulders slump as she watches Frank head for the food stand. This isn't the way it was when she and Frank first met and got married...before kids. Was it the children that changed him? After ten years of marriage, this is not her first rodeo with his quick temper. In her mind, she's forgiven him so many times, they're more than she can count. This will just be one more time, like all the rest.

"Okay kids, let's do what Daddy says. Help me get things ready for lunch."

In the distance, Cassie sees a teenager, flying on his hover-board, in front of Frank. This causes sand to swirl around her husband's knees. Although she can't hear the actual words exchanged, she can see the confrontation beginning. Frank is balancing the lunch tray and yelling at the kid. The young man yells back and offers an obscene hand gesture. He flies toward the water, blowing up sand once more.

One more step, and with his mouth trying to form a word, Frank comes to a sudden halt. His face is red and contorted. His knees buckle and he meets the ground with a thud.

Cassie watches the unfolding scene as if in slow motion. Then, lunch drops into the sand and Frank falls forward, covering it with his body.

"Frank?" whispers Cassie. The pitch in her voice rises to a scream. "What's wrong? Frank! Oh, my God!

She rushes to her husband's side and grabs for his hand. His hand and his other limbs are shrinking and drooping even as Cassie tries to hold on. The smell pouring out of Frank's remains is so powerful, she drops his hand and draws back in horror.

"Someone call 911," she yells to the gathering crowd. It's too late. Frank quickly shrivels up and dies.

Cassie hears screams coming from all around her. Other people are falling down for no apparent reason. Children are crying. She looks up and down the beach and sees people running in all directions.

"Kids, I hear sirens in the distance. Help is coming. Please hurry. Kids, you stay here with mommy. No! Don't touch Daddy."

It doesn't take much time for more bodies to be discovered; both in and out of the water. Lifeguards and emergency personnel are unsure what to do with at least a dozen corpses. Some of them are floating in the surf.

"This is the police. Get out of the water and off the beach. If you are able, go to the parking lots and wait for contact by your local beach patrol and EMS personnel. Please don't panic. We will tell you more as we learn more. Thank you. Now please, go to the parking lots or go home. Leave the bodies floating in the water alone and get to the beach fast. "

Guard-bots roll their half-tracks over the sand and announce that this is an emergency and it's time to leave the beaches. They patrol back and forth until all moving people are gone. The main headquarters of the beach patrol activates the Bots to gather all collapsed bathers and bring them to Parking Lot D, an empty lot, for inspection by the local authorities. Fortunately for them, the 'Bots' have no sense of smell.

*   *   *

We're in the finest part of town. The moving sidewalk out front is smooth and quiet as it gently transports the elite shoppers to Weatherly's Boutique. It is known for its exclusive offerings of fine ladies garments and accessories, and its equally exclusive clientele. The interior is quietly elegant. Exotic woods, imported tile and custom-made chandeliers set the mood. A Music-bot string quartet plays Mozart chamber music. The impeccably dressed, attractive staff is appropriately attentive.

The conservatively, tastefully dressed shopper says: "This dress will look perfect on my daughter. Here, look at my hologram of her wearing it. I'll take it."

The spandex-wrapped shopper next to her says: "No you won't. That dress is for me. I was just about to try it on."

"I'm sorry. What did you say?"

"I said that dress is mine. Leave it alone."

"Really? How rude!"

"Seriously? Rude? I'll give you rude, you overweight, old-money, rich bitch."

"Well, I never…"

"Give me that goddamn dress, now!"

Ms. Spandex grabs the dress in question and rips it from the elder woman's hands.

Well-dressed employees and even better dressed shoppers look at the two women embroiled in a confrontation.

"Ladies, please, we can't have such a scene in Weatherly's. It just won't do. You'll both have to leave. Madame, hand me that dress."

"The hell, you say. That dress is mine. So, give it here."

"Call security! Madame, you have to leave, now. Madame? Are you drunk? Not on our floor, please. Guard, over here, quickly."

"She's not breathing."

"She's shriveling up…her arms are shrinking; her legs are shrinking. Her body is collapsing; like an accordion."

"God, what is that noxious odor? It's coming from her."

"Run! Something's terribly wrong here. This is definitely not the way things are supposed to happen here at Weatherly's.

Someone call the authorities and the rest of you go to your respective sales stations."

* * *

"Welcome to FYI" Six-o'clock News. This is Herb Cramer sitting in for Steve Holter." Adjusting the holo-disks on his desk, he continues —

"In an unprecedented display of horror, at last count, 16 domestic planes crashed this week, throughout the country. As you can see on your holo-screen, people on the ground recorded some of these crashes. Beware, some of this footage is raw. Do not let your children view it."

Video shows a plane plunging earthward and bursting into a ball of flame. It lands nose-first and explodes upon impact. Parts of the fuselage and the interior of the plane fly in all directions. From a distance, bodies can be seen flying through the air. Smoking wreckage fills the screen. Debris is everywhere. Charred-looking bodies lie amidst still-flaming seats.

"Crowds of first-responders and locals are forming."

"I can't believe what's happening. This is terrible. My God! Look at those bodies. No. Don't. Look away! It's just too terrible to see. There's no way words can describe the horror of it all. The smell coming from some of the bodies is beyond description. One can't help but feel the severity of the situation."

"This wholesale destruction of life and property is a national tragedy. No one seems to know why. No explosions were heard. No maydays were received. The weather doesn't seem to have been a factor, either. The planes just left their designated flight paths and plunged to the ground. The NTSB is swamped. There's no way they can handle this many investigations at one time. Jim Beecher of the NTSB is here to give us some perspective on these multiple tragedies."

"Jim, what can you tell us about these plane crashes?"

"Well, Herb, in my 25 years with the NTSB, I've never seen multiple crashes like this...not even in nasty weather. We have teams on the ground in some places. But we don't have the manpower to investigate all 16 crashes at once. It'll be at least until next week to get any useful information. We'll all just have to wait further investigation. We're trying to get a handle on why so many crashes in so short a time, which is what we need Herb; more time. Not since the great war of 2030 have I seen multiple crashes like this. It just shouldn't be in peacetime."

"Thank you, Jim. Well, there you have it folks. Even the NTSB is mystified."

The screen fills once again with headshots of newscasters amidst charred ruins.

"Thousands of innocent people are dead. The crashes in the countryside and isolated landscapes are tragic, indeed. However, half the plane crashes have been in populated areas. You can see destroyed houses and damaged high-rise buildings. Fires are raging. Sirens tell of the arrival of fire trucks and their Fire-bots."

"Many of these planes crashed shortly after takeoff; their tanks filled with aviation fuel. The blazes and heat on the ground are devastating. Victims are screaming. Some are running as their skin falls off in layers. Have we been attacked? Is this war? Who are we fighting? Is this another World Trade Center attack? Could this be *War of the Worlds* for real? Your guess is as good as mine, at this point."

"The number of victims on the ground is just too numerous to calculate. Two planes crashed into schools and one can be seen smashing into a packed stadium of sports fans. The death toll must be in the tens of thousands. One plane crashes on an airport runway and skids into two other planes preparing for takeoff. Those planes also burst into flames. This has to be the worst airline tragedy in history."

* * *

"This just in—Eleven EMS units from around the country have reported female gunshot victims by their respective pilot husbands. Perhaps there's a connection to these plane crashes, although right now, I can't think of one. More news as we get it. I don't know about you folks, but I'm not flying again until this mystery is solved. Herb Cramer for FYI News signing off."

* * *

On his way, back to the office, Dave observes what the EMS personnel described and calls his boss and mentor, Nat Moyer — the short, bald, overweight, executive editor of the Daily Chronicle and 'Captain of the Fourth Estate' in this city.

"Nat, I have some news on those plane crashes. I'm talking to my vid-pad as we speak. But, let me digress here for just a minute. Wait 'til I tell you what's been going on at Sharon's morgue. She's never seen anything like it, and frankly, neither have I."

"You'll do that and more, Dave. I just received word that Blake Eldridge has died. He passed away from something unusual. It happened this morning. No time for details now. You do realize what this means...Dave, my boy, you are now our lead reporter."

"Wait a minute, Nat. I can't just jump in and replace Blake. He's the Chronicle's golden boy. He's famous. He's my idol."

"Dave, if you don't stop twirling your mustache, you're going to tear it right off your face. Just calm down and listen to me."

"Don't you realize what you've been doing with Blake since you left the mailroom. Well, now it's time for you to do what Blake taught you."

"Marge, feel free to jump in here anytime."

"This is Marge, Dave. Listen to me. I know Blake, and I know what he wanted. Blake let it be known that you were his protégé. You were his chosen one to take over if he was ever unable to do his job. Well, now he can't do his job. I don't mean to sound cold, but that's the way it is."

"What do you think you've been doing all these years at Blake's side? I'll tell you what—you've been preparing for just this sort of situation. So, you get out there and investigate. Sorry to go on like this."

"As long as you remember that it's not about the news; it's about people, you'll be fine. That was Blake's strength. He never forgot that life happens to people. Show how the facts effect people and you have a story that matters. Dave, Nat and I know that you care about people. Stick to that, focus on people and people will care about what you write. Facts and people. Do that and you'll be honoring Blake properly."

"Dave, before I went off to college, I lived on a farm. On the farm, you learn that good or bad, you deal with whatever happens. A horse gives birth and a cow gets slaughtered for dinner. Things happen. Things beyond your control."

"If I may, Marge, let me jump in here". says Nat. "This is not the time to be modest or unsure, Dave. Blake and I have been mentoring you for years for this kind of situation. Trust me when I say: 'you can do this'. You're ready. Fate has unexpectedly ushered you into a higher position. Don't hesitate. Pounce on this as the opportunity of a lifetime."

"Nat, ten minutes ago, I was content to ride on Blake's coat tails...but now, everything is different."

"Not so different, Dave. You've been rehearsing for this for a long time. Blake's been preparing you for this. I've been preparing you for this. Marge has been preparing you for this. It's your time in the spotlight. Take it. This could be the break of a lifetime. Now get out there and investigate this rash of unusual deaths and report back to me ASAP. And, by-the-way, unless those plane crashes you're investigating are connected to these deaths, put them on the back burner."

"Alright Nat. If you think I can do this, I'll do it. Call you later. Bye, and thanks for your vote of confidence, both of you."

*   *   *

A short time later — "Listen to me, Nat, I couldn't have imagined what I'm witnessing. When I came through here yesterday, the moving sidewalks and streets were crowded with people...active people; people rushing here and there. Look at your holo-screen. I'm downtown and seeing for myself what's been happening. First, those plane crashes reported on the AP, and now, tragedy here, only not with planes. There are dead bodies all over the city."

"The Trash-bots can't keep up with the profusion of remains. Sharon's morgue is overrun with corpses, too. Something horrible is happening. I'll let you know what I find. Are there any reports of starved cadavers showing up, anywhere else?"

"What do you know that I don't?" asks Nat. What do you know about the corpses? Is Sharon giving you inside info? Check your scanner. Ours is reporting multiple, mysterious deaths."

"Sharon is the reason I'm here. The only inside info I have from her is what I saw in her lab. Something weird is going on and I intend to find out what. At this point I don't know how big this will get. I don't know if there is a connection between the multiple planes crashes and these cadavers in our city. Whatever else I've been assigned, you've put me as lead investigator on this story. Now I think I can handle this."

"I know you can handle this, Dave. Stop adjusting your tie-knot and concentrate. There may be danger out there, but this is the breakout story you've been waiting for. It's the one I've been waiting for, too. So, get out there and investigate and report. Think Pulitzer, my boy, think Pulitzer."

* * *

"Jack, this is the movie I told you about. This is what I call an action film. Ooo-whee! Between the special effects and the 3-D Holo-Imax, it's like we're in the film, not just watching it. I take that back — we are in this film. This is great. This is state of the art filmmaking. I could swear that fist was gonna hit me. I saw you. You flinched, too."

"I told you this was a terrific movie. Now aren't you glad you listened to me?" "You were right. I promise I'll never doubt you again. Now shut up, have some popcorn, and let me enjoy the rest of the movie. Damn, it's good."

"Look over there, about three rows down. I don't believe it. How could anybody sleep through a movie like this? Look at that guy two seats away from us. He's the one who pushed his way in front of us when we got tickets. Wait a minute. Look at the lady in front of us. What the hell is going on here? Whoa! Do you smell that? Something weird is going on here."

"I don't think we should stay here. Run Jack!"

"I'm right behind you."

"Holy shit! Jack, do you see what I see? People, no, bodies, all over the lobby. Let's get the car and get the hell out of here."

*   *   *

The bus carrying 53 seniors to the casino is clean, modern and quite impressive. Henry, the bus driver is older than many other drivers, but thoroughly seasoned to transporting seniors to casinos, dinner-theaters and shopping trips.

"Henry, how much longer 'til we get to the casino?"

"We're right on schedule, ma'am. I'd say in about 45 minutes we should be there. Until we arrive, please take advantage of your holo-screen located in the headrest of the seat in front of you. It offers books, magazines, news and hundreds of channels...all in 3-D. Watch something and before you know it, we'll be at the casino."

"We'll just enjoy the scenery, Henry. Thank you."

"Evie, Tell us about your last cruise. Where did you go?"

"We went to the Caribbean on that new ship. You know, the one with 15,000 passengers. It was wonderful. We wined and dined for 10 days. You may as well take advantage of this wonderful ship, now. The way technology is leaping forward; we won't be traveling much anymore."

"Why do you say that?"

"Lily, Virtual Reality entertainment has reached the point where we no longer have to go anywhere...except to our favorite casino, of course. You just plug in and you're anywhere you want to be. You can even experience trips to the past or the future. All of this can be experienced at your local theater and, one day soon, in your own home."

"That's true. You can be anywhere, anytime and, it feels real."

"Did you see the putt on that last hole? That's what I call 'scratch golf.'"

"Don't I know it. I'm happy to see this generation having some interest in traditional sports. It's good for them and good for society. They need to earn the fruits of hard work and the healthy benefits of refined competition."

"You mean, not like we play at the country club?"

"Ha, ha. Very funny. We do just fine for old duffers. Nothing beats fresh air and the comradery of the nineteenth hole."

"Caroline, why don't you join in the conversation? We'll be at the casino soon. Caroline? Hey Caroline, what's wrong?"

"Oh my God! Look at her. If, that's really her? Evie, come see. Something's happened to Caroline. Do the rest of you smell an awful smell?"

"Rosie! No, Rosie. Damn! What's happening?"

"Henry, pull this bus over to the side of the road. Something bad is going on here. Henry? I said pull over."

"Henry, stop the goddamn bus! Somebody get up to the front of the bus and get Henry to stop right now."

"People. People. Hold on! We're gonna' crash."

Henry, the bus driver, dies before the bus crashes. Of the 53 passengers on board the bus, 39 survive the crash. Of these survivors, 9 drop dead outside the bus and shrivel up. The remaining 30 seniors hug each other and cry for those lost.

"911. 911. Hurry! Get our location from my watch-cell. Our bus has crashed and we have dead and injured on the ground. Please, hurry! My God! What a smell. I think it's coming from the bodies on the ground. Let's move away from them."

* * *

"This is Kyle Trent of Station 4 News. I'm here in front of the courthouse interviewing members of the anti-abortion faction. The crowd numbers in the hundreds. The hover-buses are bringing more protestors by the minute. This is getting out of hand quickly. I've never seen both sides so angry with each other. It's getting downright scary. Opponents are holding signs that say: 'Kill the Baby Killers' If that doesn't show how far apart these two groups are, I don't know what does. People are cursing and yelling at each other. Fists are raised and the chanting is getting louder."

"Killing babies is just plain wrong. I dare you to show our side on your program. It's God's will that the evil abortionists be stopped. Haven't they ever read the Bible? Satan is here, in our midst. We will defeat them." she curses, pointing at the pro-choice group gathered across the street.

"Soulless murderers should die. You can't play God with no consequences."

"You sons of Satan. You daughters of the devil. May you all rot in hell!"

*   *   *

"Over to you, Marcie."

"Thanks, Kyle."

"This is Marcie Pembroke of Station-4 News. I'm here with Nancy Dale of the Pro-Choice Movement. Nancy, what is it that your group wants?"

"Well Marcie, all we want is freedom to choose for the mother. No government and no religion has the right to interfere in a pregnant mother's right to choose. It's inhumane. Besides, the rich have their designer-babies. The rest of us should have the choice to have our babies, designer or not. Those bastards over there claim that we are playing God. They are the ones who want to tinker with genes and DNA to make 'perfect' babies. They're the ones playing God! she screams. They better get out of our way. We will defeat them. Watch out! That guy's got a gun."

"Hey, lady. Get up. You get outta my way. Lady? She's not breathing. Somebody help! Oh, my God! Look at her! She's shriveling up. What the hell's going on here?"

"Kyle? Are you seeing what I'm seeing? Are people dropping to the ground where you are? Something's really wrong here. I didn't hear any shots, did you? Call 911. Keep the cameras rolling. My God! People are collapsing as we speak. The smell is rancid. I can't stand it. It's. It's. I don't know what it is. Help! This is Marcie Pembroke of Station-4 News, signing off."

* * *

Death has crept up and is smothering all parts of Dave's beloved city. His driverless car expertly swerves around bodies lying in the road. The city looks like the setting for a major motion picture horror movie. He comes to an intersection with numerous cadavers on the sidewalks and in the streets. The moving sidewalks have stopped; jammed up by throngs of cadavers. A screaming child stands on the sidewalk next to a shriveled body.

Dave exits his car and embraces the child.

"Hi, what's your name? I see your mommy has fallen and can't get up.

"My name's Carl and my mommy's sick. Mommy's real sick. She needs a doctor."

"You're right, mommy needs help. Come with me and we'll see if we can find a doctor to help her."

"Thank you, mister. I want mommy to get up and take me home. Let's get a doctor."

Carefully avoiding contact with the woman's body, Dave grabs the woman's purse for ID.

* * *

A shell-shocked woman shuffles by and tries to maneuver over and around the corpses. A few people are kneeling over what looks like shrunken bodies. The one kneeling has a hand or handkerchief over his/her nose.

Dave stops again and hustles the woman into his car and drives until he spots some uniforms patrolling.

"Madam, you'll be safe here. These officers will help you. Just tell them what happened. Officer, please help this boy. His name is Carl and his mother just collapsed a few blocks from here. Here is her purse. I'm a reporter with the Daily Chronicle. I'm pursuing this story, now."

"Thanks. We'll take care of the boy and the woman. You be careful out there."

"Oh, one last thing, don't touch any of these bodies. We don't yet know if they're contagious."

"Thanks, you be careful, too."

* * *

"Marge, I'm giving you a live report from my vid-glasses, as I make my way to the office. Tell Nat that something so awful it's almost indescribable is happening as we speak, that it is unprecedented. Masses of people are dying in the streets. More people than I can count. I'm so sorry. All I can do is report. I wish I could help them."

"The good news, if there is such a thing at this point, as you can see, is that not all people are affected. For every afflicted person, I see two or three still standing. How can this plague affect some of us and not others? There must be a common denominator."

"A collie and a German shepherd are walking by. Apparently, this, whatever this is, has no effect on dogs. I see cats, too. They look healthy, and on the prowl. Pigeons are flying around, so that lets them out. Yet, with no warning and without a sound, people are quickly and quietly collapsing. This is, without a doubt, the scariest, strangest story I've ever encountered. I wish Blake was here to work with me. Of all times to die, his timing couldn't be worse."

* * *

"I'm going over to the park now. Follow my video. Would you look at that? The lake is beautiful and tranquil as usual. Ducks are flying or floating and pets are running free. Wait a minute. I see people in the floatboats and some are slumped over. Others, not infected, are screaming or crying. Except for that big kid by the pond, feeding the swans, kids don't seem to be affected, either."

"My God! Marge, look at all the bodies on the grass. These people look as if they were just sitting, having a picnic just a short while ago. Those not affected are the picture of helplessness. Make sure Nat sees my transmissions."

"Have your 'holo-pic' taken with a Ranger-bot. I can take your holo-pic for you. Do you want food? We Ranger-bots are here to serve."

"Marge, look in the sky. There must be a news-drone for every news service up there. If we have any edge on them, it's my connection to Sharon at the morgue. I better keep reporting."

* * *

"I'm here at the ball field. Marge, do you see the bodies scattered all over the infield? I'm panning over to the stands. Two spectators are fighting now and, oh my God! They just collapsed onto each other. Other sports fans are slumped over or on the ground, and do you see the people crying? Listen to the children screaming. I don't know what brought these people down, but it's quick and silent. Cadavers don't decompose this quickly. Even I know that. Yet, that's the smell coming from them. The air is ripe with panic."

A young couple hurries by, crying and holding each other. Other people are scattering in all directions.

"We have to get home. The kids will be frantic worrying about us. I knew we shouldn't have come into the city today. I just had a feeling."

"Don't worry, dear. We'll be home soon. I'll call the kids right now and tell them."

"I can't hear you over the screaming and crying. What are you saying? Several of our staff are dead...at the office? Oh, Marge, I'm so sorry. This just keeps getting worse by the minute. I'll see you soon."

*   *   *

"Nat, follow along with me. I don't want to do this. You know me and my claustrophobia. Maybe I'll just wait up here on the street and interview people as they exit the subway."

"No way, Dave. you have to go down into the subway. I know you're claustrophobic, but the news comes first. The public needs to know that you're on the scene. Now get down there and report." says Marge.

"Okay, Marge. I'm inching my way down the stairs. See all the corpses? They're more than I can count. I'm in the tunnel leading to the subway platform. I'm having trouble breathing."

"Stay with it, Dave. You're doing just fine."

I don't know how I'm going to do this. I'm so scared. Damn claustrophobia. It's beaten me before, but I can't let it defeat me today. I need this story...I have to go wherever it takes me.

"Help me! Some big guy just fell on me and he has me pinned against a bench. Oh, man, he's shrinking. Now I can push him off me. Damn, what an odor. I have to get out of here. The walls are closing in on me. I can't breathe."

"Calm down, Dave. I need you to continue recording the scene in the subway. Breathe, deeply. You can do this. Close your eyes and breathe...deep breaths. That's good. Now, open your eyes and show us what's happening."

"Nat, as I pan around, record all this and maybe later we'll assess how many bodies are on the platform. One hover-train is stopped. I can hear its quiet motor running. Look at all those bodies in the train and blocking the doorways. The smell down here is so bad, so rancid, I've got to go topside. Follow me back up. Survivors are gathered around the subway entrance and on the platforms, not knowing what to do."

"Dave, you be careful. I know you're not just a reporter; you're an investigative reporter. But, that being said, your health and safety come first."

"Thanks for your concern, Nat. I'm inclined to agree with the EMS guys I spoke with earlier; I don't think this, whatever it is, is contagious. I don't yet know how it selects its victims, but, just to play safe, I'm not touching any bodies, and I think I can continue to explore."

"Sorry sir. I think it's best if you walk up to the street level and catch a breath of fresh air. Here, take my hand...I'll walk with you."

"How can you be so cold to just record this tragedy? says the man. Doesn't the horror of all this get to you?"

Yes, sir, the horror of all this does get to me. But, I'm just doing my job by recording this for the Chronicle. There will probably be a special edition out later today. Perhaps my reporting will help people to understand what's happening and how to deal with it."

"Sorry, Mr. Reporter, I don't mean to blame you. It's just so horrible and I don't know what to do. Thanks for your help. I can go on from here. You be careful, now. Bye."

Dave leaves the man standing, wide-eyed, at the subway entrance. The man has tears in his eyes and seems to not know which direction to go. As he emerges from the subway entrance, others exit the subway right behind him. Between the intense odor coming from the subway and the bright sunlight, all seem a little disoriented at their arrival topside.

* * *

Dave captures a full-color hologram of the horror of the city. Shriveled bodies of mostly adults are his main focus. They all appear to have been stopped in their tracks.

"Nat, as you can see, the bodies; no, the remains of peoples' bodies, lie all over the city — on sidewalks, in doorways, at subway entrances, at ATM machines, in cars, at bus stops, crossing the street...everywhere. "

"Here and there, a survivor can be seen darting into or out of a building. The nature of these deaths is still a mystery. The infection is so quick that no cries of pain are heard. There seems to be no defense against it."

My city is dying. We're being attacked, but by whom, and why? How long can this attack last? Where is it coming from?

With enough footage for now, Dave heads back to his desk at The Chronicle.

*   *   *

"Nat, Marge, both of you. Look at your vid-screens. Rioting and looting have broken out. People are smashing store windows and grabbing whatever they can get and running away."

"Hey you. You do know what you're doing is wrong."

"What's it to you? You're no cop."

"No, I'm a reporter.

"Yeah. Well get lost. This is none of your business."

"I just want to know why you're doing this. You could get hurt. You could get arrested. You could go to jail. Why risk all that just to steal something?"

"If you were in my place, you'd do the same damn thing. You're no better than me. Three months ago, I had a good job. Then, without warning, I was laid off. What am I supposed to do? I have a wife and kids. You want a story for your paper, I'll give you one. People shouldn't be thrown away, like garbage. People need to be able to live. You think I'm wrong. Hell, the society that puts me in a desperate situation like this, they're the ones who are wrong."

"Now, you got your story and I've got to get something I can use or sell. Get away from me." says the looter.

"Please, I don't want to see you busted or shot. Here is all the money I have on me right now. Take it and get out of here before the shooting starts. Buy what you need and go home to your family."

"I don't know what to say. Thank you...and bless you."

As the grateful man disappears around the corner of the building, a man with a hammer in his hand, approaches that same store window.

"You get the hell away from my store. Get out of here. Don't you touch that window. You come any closer and I'll kill you. You hear me? The cops are on their way. Get out of here."

"Oh my God! Nat, look at your screen. That shop keeper just shot that looter. This is insane."

"Some of these same people are being struck down by the plague. Some of them are attacking the Cop-bots that show up to quell the riots."

"Bots and rioters are battling it out. Rioters with pipes, baseball bats and even trashcans are bashing Bots. The Bots are built to take punishment and are immune to threats and insults. However, they are quickly outnumbered."

"Boy, it doesn't take long for chaos to run free. All you need is an interruption in our normal routine, and people go crazy. More Bots are arriving now. I hear shooting from far away. As you can see, Bots and looters are lying in the street and on the sidewalk. They all look dead."

"Dave, you're right around the corner from the office, so get up here now. We don't need any more footage, but we do need you to be safe. I'm your boss, and I'm telling you to get your butt up here now."

* * *

"I'm on my way. Nat, view this live report, ASAP. My car is driving into the parking lot of the Daily Chronicle. Several cars are partway into parking spaces. I'm pulling into a spot and starting to check partially parked cars. As you can see, the occupants are either slumped over in their seats or in a heap on the floor. Bodies cover the parking lot itself."

"Ma'am, please stop screaming. I know, I know; the horror of all this can't be exaggerated. Please, don't stay in your car. Go upstairs to the Chronicle office. Go to the fourth floor and ask for Marge. Please, you can't stay here. It's not safe. Nat, are you getting this? Nine bodies in seven cars; all emaciated. Fifteen or twenty victims on the ground in the parking lot. Thanks to the cars being driverless, none of the cars or property are damaged."

"Young man, are you sure they will let me in? I don't know anybody at your newspaper."

"Yes, ma'am. I'm speaking with them now. What is your name?

"My name is Phyllis."

"Go upstairs, Phyllis. I'm telling them you're coming. The fourth floor. The Daily Chronicle. Go now."

* * *

"Before I come upstairs, Nat, I'm going to check the immediate neighborhood. Look at this long view, up and down the street. Bodies line the streets in both directions, but no cars have run onto the sidewalks. You're seeing what I'm seeing but, do you realize that there isn't a sound; just an eerie quiet."

"A dog is running around in circles. It's probably overwhelmed by the smell coming from the bodies. I have to tread lightly here. It's like walking through a minefield. Can you see the bodies in piles in almost every store on the block? The grotesqueness of this situation is only exceeded by the immensity of the body count. Neither can be overstated."

"Nat, I'm sending you on-the-spot coverage of the horror in our city. It's unlike anything I've ever seen or read about. The magnitude of this catastrophe is beyond comprehension. As far as the eye can see, death has triumphed. What was recently a bustling metropolis of lively crowds has been reduced to human rubble on a massive scale. Hawks are flying or pecking at the corpses. The accompanying odor is so intense; I sometimes feel like I'm going to faint. What do you think?"

"I think you may be right to keep recording what's happening, as it's happening. You know what? If you feel up to it, skip rushing up to the office for now. You're our reporter on the scene. Keep exploring. I'm monitoring what you're seeing. Keep your vid-cam on. Marge and I are viewing every minute of video from you. I have the holo-screens and e-news on hold. Drop any other work you have and concentrate on this event. I know this may sound cold and uncaring, but maybe we can scoop the other papers. This tragedy is unquestionably terrible, but, remember our news media motto — 'If it bleeds, it leads'."

"Over here, Nat. Look at this shriveled body sitting in a barber chair; as though waiting for a haircut. This person; this victim, didn't even have time to get out of the chair. Two other patrons and a barber are slumped in chairs and on the floor. The unending supply of holo-zines are scattered all over the floor."

"Nat, my God! I see two people collapsing now. Look at your monitor. There's no blood, no sound and no cries for help. They just collapse, like a puppet with all its strings cut at once. This is the story, in real time. They just drop in their tracks; like a balloon person with the air suddenly let out. Nat, I think these people are dead before they hit the ground. My guess is that they never knew what hit them. And those of us left standing; we just don't know what to do. I just want to help them."

I thought the anguish and pain of my series on handicapped children was terrible...and it was. But this, this is off the charts. I never imagined I'd be covering a story this shocking and gut-wrenching. Blake, where are you when I need you?

* * *

"What about putting Doc Malone on this? He's our science guy. What does he make of all this?"

"Did you forget? Doc is in Europe on assignment. He's not scheduled to return until the end of the week. I'm sorry, Dave, but you're on your own on this one. The dangers are clear and present, but the rewards will be equal to the dangers. You're the Chronicle's number one reporter on the street. Welcome to the majors, my boy. This is the big one. You can do it. I have faith in you."

* * *

"The streets, the shops, the restaurants, the theaters and museums that once gave a warm sense of place like no other, are gone. Now, death and more death, has colored everything and every place. These new, foul sights and smells have spoiled and suffocated our once beautiful and vibrant city. I don't know about you, but I, for one, am not prepared to witness the death of our city…not today…not any day. This just can't be the end."

* * *

"Branson's jewelry store, next to Beaner's Coffee shop, shows a salesman, his arms spread over a showcase, looking burned beyond recognition. On closer inspection, it's clear that these bodies are not burned. One of the customers, with a watch glistening in the light, appears to be a pile of charred remains…shriveled, not burned. Sharon says they are not burned — shriveled, wilted, shrunken, yes…but not burned."

"Lady, are you all right? ma'am, please talk to me. I think she's in shock. Nat, call 911 and alert them, although I would think that the authorities already know what's happening. Ma'am, the EMS personnel and the police are on their way, right now. If you'll just sit here, by the door, they'll be here soon. I promise. I'll stay with you until they come."

"Nat, what was called 'shell-shock' after WWI and PTSD after Vietnam, is what I'm witnessing here, now. This woman represents most of the survivors I've seen today. I don't blame them. If it weren't for my studies in Eastern philosophy and the fact that I have a job to do, I probably would be in shock right now too. I can't make any sense of what's happening either. We have 'zombies' roaming the city; although in this instance, they don't present a danger to others."

* * *

"Sterling's Haberdashery, the up-scale clothing store near the Chronicle building, has new-suited corpses in various poses. A large, crumpled body in a checked vest is lying on the floor. No one alive seems to be present and the doors are wide open. I'm scanning the rear of the store. As you can see, more bodies are in the back. Several remains are in the dressing rooms. If it weren't for the shriveling up, it would resemble the St. Valentine's Day massacre."

"Mr., uh Randall, I see by your nametag, your name is Randall. Is there anything I can do for you? Do you need help getting up? Can I help you get someplace?"

"Thank you. No, I'm okay. I guess I just blanked out. Between the dead bodies and the smell, I just couldn't take it. I work here. I don't know what's going on. Do you?"

"No, I'm afraid I don't. I'm a reporter investigating this terrible situation. Can you tell me anything that might shed some light on what's happened here?"

"No. This nightmare is a mystery to me. I'm scared. I don't know whether to wait here or to go home. I should be with my family."

"If I were you, I'd head home right now and try not to touch any of these corpses."

"Thank you. I think I'll do just that." Bye."

* * *

"Nat, the lunch crowd at Beaner's Coffee Shop is scattered all around the interior and at the umbrella-covered tables outside. Some are seated, but most are on the ground. Coffee cups peek out from under shriveled remains or lie next to them. The ratio seems to be three males to every female. This disarray of cadavers suggests something immediate; not gradual."

"Ma'am, you were here before this tragedy started. Is that correct?"

"Yes, that was just about an hour ago. I was sitting here with one of my co-workers. We come here almost every day, for a short break. I recognize others from our office. At least, I think I do. Do you know why this is happening?"

"No, I'm sorry, I don't. I work at The Daily Chronicle around the corner. I'm a reporter. Is there anything you can tell me about this tragedy...anything at all?"

"I don't know anything. I went to the ladies' room to freshen up. I got a call on my cellphone, and when I returned, not more than ten minutes later, people were already on the ground. I never heard a thing."

"I'm going to my office at The Chronicle. Would you like to come with me?"

"Thank you, but no. I'm going across the street to our office to tell them what happened. This is terrible, just terrible."

Trash-bots skitter around the entire neighborhood pushing bodies into sloppy piles. Being robots, they don't understand the word "desecration" but what else is to be done? They're doing what they're programmed to do.

"Look at this policeman and two construction workers, all dead. And here, a delivery truck with three bodies on the ramp leading up to the rear of the truck. A window washer's remains hang down from a scaffold. A Traffic-bot seems rooted to the middle of the street in a futile attempt to direct traffic. It turns this way and that trying to clear a clogged intersection.

"Nat, are you watching?"

"Dave."

"Not now, Marge. Just watch."

"Dave."

"Watch and then we'll talk."

"Dave!"

"What's so important that you have to interrupt my vid-cam report?"

"That's the problem, Dave. We are only receiving the audio portion of your transmission. The video portion is dead."

"What? No video? Now what?"

"You'll have to report as if you're writing the story. You know, take notes that will be transcribed later. Like the old days. Start now, and when you get here we'll give you a new vid-cam."

"Dammit! This is some of the best footage I've ever shot. This is so old school. I guess it's better than nothing. Describe and Write."

"After seeing our immediate neighborhood, I have lots of questions and no answers. There is no obvious reason for what is taking place. Sharon's morgue is filled with emaciated bodies similar to what I'm showing you here. You know she's the science expert in our household, and she can't figure out what's going on. It's just beyond belief. Nat, I'll call you when I have more for you.

I'll just write up a little extra copy before heading up to the office. Bye."

*   *   *

"Sharon, I only have a few minutes here. Listen, Blake Eldridge has died. It sounds like from something that you observed in your morgue. I don't have time to investigate his death because now Nat's made me the lead reporter for the Chronicle. I'm taking over for Blake."

"Oh Dave, that's wonderful. I liked Blake, but if anyone at the Chronicle deserves to take over for him, it's you. I'm proud of you. Be careful, and get out there and show them all what you can do."

"Sharon, I just wanted to call you and give you an update on these weird deaths. Do you really think I can do this; I mean take over for Blake?"

"Dave, I have every confidence in your ability as a reporter. You've worked hard and you've become an outstanding reporter. Blake would be proud of you. Nat's proud of you. I'm proud of you. So yes, you can do this. Without a doubt."

"What you have going on in your morgue is just the tip of the iceberg that I'm seeing all over the city. Emaciated carcasses identical to those in your morgue are blanketing our town, both indoors and out. It's the most bizarre event I've ever witnessed. At first there were only a few. Then, quickly, the body count began to rise, and it's rising by the minute. There must be a common denominator; why some are struck down and others spared. There must be a reason."

"What does Doc Malone have to say about all this?"

"His timing stinks. He's in Europe on assignment. He's not due back until the end of the week. That leaves you and me to figure this out. Unofficially, you're now the lead science expert on this event. Okay? I know you can do this. You graduated at the top of your class. You've always been an over-achiever. Now is the time for over-achieving. Forget Doc. You're in charge now."

Dave continues: "I'll keep in touch and keep you informed. But, at this point, I'm as mystified as you. The only thing I seem to have found is that it's unlikely that whatever is responsible for this mass death is airborne. Also, it's not out to get all of us. And, it doesn't seem to have any effect on animals or birds. The trees and plants in the park look unaffected, too."

"At first, these deaths seemed like isolated incidents of random anomalies. But now, after seeing so many corpses, in different locales, in so short a time, I'm convinced these deaths are neither random nor isolated. A very scary pattern is beginning to emerge here. Something we haven't yet isolated is selecting and killing some of us, but not all of us. Although non-whites outnumber whites, race doesn't seem to be a factor. This plague knows who it wants."

"Sharon, have you found out anything else that would shed light on the cause of this, I guess the most appropriate word is, plague.?"

"No Dave, still not a clue. We're running tests on all the bodies here in the lab, but no success yet. We have to get to the bottom of this. Think of all the children at our hospital. What's to become of them? Please be careful."

"Be well, my dear. I love you very much, and I will continue to investigate. Keep me informed of any progress in your lab. Oh, I almost forgot; this wasting away is so quick, I'm sure death is total before the bodies hit the ground. Bye for now."

"One more thing, Dave; since you left this morning, five more bodies have been brought in; all in the same condition as the others. I'm out of freezers and have stacked them in the basement. Nothing in medical school prepared me for this. At this point, I can't think of anything that acts as quickly as what you describe. Please be careful, but continue to keep me updated. Just in case this is contagious, please don't touch anyone. Love you. Bye."

*   *   *

"Marge, it's me again. I'm downstairs in the lobby. Look at this body in the doorway. It's keeping the door open. I don't know whether to touch it or not. Oh, wait, Sharon warned me not to touch anybody. You won't believe what I'm seeing here. Check your holo-screen. Mine is down. Three of our staff members are lying on the floor. At least I think it's them. One of them looks like Josh, our sportswriter. Poor Josh. He's so young and he just got married last year. It's not fair dammit. It's hard to tell when they're so shriveled up."

"One of them looks like Marty, our ever-bitter security guard. Another resembles Eric, our copy editor. No loss there —

Eric, you S.O.B. You kept me down for years. You made sure I didn't get to be a real reporter. You made it clear to me that without a college degree, you felt I didn't deserve to be a reporter. You did your best to make me feel small and unworthy. You must have flipped when I became an assistant investigative reporter. And a few years later, when Blake picked me to be his assistant, you must have gone out of your mind. Well, look at you now. I finally get to write about you. You're lucky Blake taught me to be impartial; not to judge. I will honor him by giving you a break you don't deserve. I know it's wrong to gloat, but I just can't forgive you, Eric. Good bye and good riddance.

"I'll be right up. Jesus! Marge, there are two dead people in the elevator. God what an odor...like ozone and rotten meat. This is just crazy."

*   *   *

The ride up in the elevator is foul. Dave has to put his handkerchief over his nose. He stands rail straight, not wanting to make contact with either of the bodies in the elevator. When he emerges from the elevator, Marge greets him in tears.

She, too, has a handkerchief over her nose. Dave embraces her shaking body and tries to comfort her. Whether it's Marge crying or the impact of all that he's seen in the past few hours, tears well up in Dave's eyes, too. The immensity of the situation is beyond human understanding and acceptance.

"Dave, I don't know what's happening. Help me out here. Stan, Peter and 'Grumpy Ron' are all dead. Paula and Deb are also dead. I know you said not to touch any of the bodies, but we have to move them. We're putting all the cadavers in the men's room. We don't know what else to do. Words erupt from Marge like a burst from an automatic weapon — What did you find? What's happening? What do I tell people when they call the Chronicle? Nat's in his office. He wants to see you. Oh, God, I just want to go home."

Willy and Harold struggle by carrying bodies to the men's room. Dave refrains from telling them not to touch any bodies. Natalie, one of the papers legal consultants, follows, cleaning up after them. A clutter-free workplace now means body-free.

"You guys can stay and help Nat if you want. We can use all the help we can get...seeing as how short-handed we've just become. But, if you want to go home to be with your families, go now and don't worry about the office. We'll be fine here."

Unaware of the meaning of the commotion, 'Foodie', the office Snack-bot, glides by offering food and drink to all present, including one of the new corpses. Marge, the former cool, calm and cynical helmsman of the entire newspaper, is as frantic as Dave's wife, Sharon. She can't stop talking and she can't stop shaking —

"Don't worry, Marge. I promise you, we'll get to the bottom of this. We will find out why this is happening. Now, sit at your desk and when the phone rings, tell people that we are aware of the situation and are already looking into it. Tell them to look in the Chronicle, tomorrow, for more information. That's all we can do for now. I'll work with Nat and we'll plan our strategy for tomorrow's edition."

"Can you do that, Marge? Nat and I need you to handle the front desk; now more than ever. The Chronicle needs you. Please, help us to help you."

"Okay, Dave. I feel better, now that you're here. I'll be at my desk, and thanks."

*　*　*

"Herb Cramer of FYI News at Six, here, with an update — Heads of state, high-ranking military officers, captains of industry and more than half of all power brokers, politicians and leaders in their fields are gone; victims of this plague. Their collective demise has been swift and thorough. Who will step in to replace them remains to be seen.

This is just insane. The beginning of this week, all these people were alive and well."

"The World Bank, The Fed and Wall Street are all in crisis. More than half of their top officers have succumbed to this most vicious of epidemics. Mac Stranger, Lanny Spanberg, Wolf Paulowitz and Larry Arvett are but a handful of those connected to 'big money.' They have all suddenly disappeared from the economics scene. When it comes to doing business as usual, overnight "Big Government" and "Big Money" have crashed and burned. These insulated and wealthy 'one-per-centers' have become victims of this plague, just like the rest of us."

"Those not caught in the clutches of whatever this is are roaming the sidewalks or drinking or just sitting, looking shell-shocked. Did any of you see anything? Did any of you hear anything? Were any shots fired? What is that terrible smell?"

"This just in from Hollywood – Actors of renown —Warner Brett, Allison Dolly, Kenny Gerard, Annie Jenson, Peter Blanda, Nancy Nelly and the list just goes on and on. Celebrity after celebrity has succumbed to this cruel epidemic. Boyd Flynn and his entire country band are also victims, as are Lady Clarice and Mindy Crawford."

"Performers in all fields, writers, producers, filmmakers, agents, and a variety of others in the entertainment field have been reported victims of this insidious plague. Reality holo-gram personalities, talk-show hosts, soap stars, even newscasters and political pundits of all persuasions are gone. We have lost some of our most talented people."

"The art scene mourns the loss of the painter, Peter Casso, and prima ballerina Madison Shorter. Symphony conductor, Wesley

James, and Opera star Vincenzo Brittoni, have all perished. Ernesto Fuersa Paz, this year's winner of the Nobel Prize for literature, and Antoine Gaudi, this year's recipient of the Nobel prize in physics, are also gone."

"We are quickly losing some of our best and brightest stars. Our pool of talented people is dwindling as we speak. How do we replace these great talents? God help those of us left. Who could have suspected that this week would unfold like this?"

"As the numbers are updated and more details are available, fans of all ages, colors, ethnic backgrounds and religious orientations are paying their respects at these stars' Hollywood residences and their Walk of Fame markers. Crowds are gathering and people are in tears. Makeshift shrines are popping up everywhere. Their idols, mentors and entertainers of choice, are no longer with us."

"Apparently, money and power are useless in fighting this illness. Prior good health means nothing to this affliction. Age doesn't seem to matter, either. We all seem to be at the mercy of this plague. I'm crushed and heartbroken by this massive loss of talent. Herb Cramer signing off."

* * *

"Yo, dude. You know you ain't supposed to be in our 'hood. So, what you doin' here?"

"This ain't your 'hood, bro. This is *Corner Guys* turf. You dig?

"You got to be kidding...or stupider than you look. *Uptown* owns this corner and that one over there and that one over there. You *Corner Guys* is outta your territory and outta your place."

"You think you can scare me, punk? You dumber than you look."

With a wave of his arm, one of the *Corner Guys* raises his hand and eight more like himself; all packing, come out of the surrounding buildings. At the same time, ten *Uptown* guys race up in two, large, 'tricked-out, hover-trucks'.

Just before the standoff escalates into warfare, gang members on both sides start to fall and shrivel up. In less than a minute, eleven corpses lie on the ground. Not a shot was fired. It's an unusually quiet resolution to the ongoing conflict of turf warfare. Those not infected, run away as fast as they can.

Slowly at first, and then more and more, the people who live in this most violent of neighborhoods, come out of their houses and view the scene.

"Halle, you see what happened?"

"No, I ain't seen nothin'."

"What the hell is that smell?"

"Hey, Rosalie, you seen anything?"

"Hell no. When I see them boys get together on the corner, I go hide in my house. I ain't gettin' shot just for lookin' out my window."

"Edward, you know some o' them boys. You know what happened here?"

"Damn, that smell is bad. I mean real bad."

"Not me. I seen nothin'. Them 'bangers' just gettin' it on like always. Only, I don't heard nothin' either. Man, them guys just whacked each other wit no sound."

"So, ain't nobody seen nothin' and nobody hear nothin' and they all be dead. Just like that. Somethin' strange goin' on here. Scary shit goin' on here."

"I can't take that smell no mo'. I'm goin home."

"This is Cop-bot #23, on the scene. I am at Twelfth and 3rd Streets. I am securing the crime scene for a human officer. I am keeping all civilians behind the tape. There will be no contamination on my watch. 10-4, over and out."

*   *   *

"Hey, get back in your own lane! Get outta my lane. Son-of-a-bitch! Did you see that? That asshole just hit that car and rammed the guardrail. Jake, that car's on fire. Look in the other lane. I don't believe it. This is like a Hollywood movie. Jake, what are you doing? Straighten out or we're gonna be in an accident. Look out! That truck almost hit us. Jake, what's the matter with you? Wake up! Aarrrgh!"

*   *   *

"This is Gary Curdy here at Corporate Stadium, folks. This is the first game of the 2040 World Soccer Playoffs. The weather is beautiful. 140,000 soccer fans are here with me. With English, the universal language now, all sports fans feel equal. The fans have been waiting for this match all season...they're pumped. Food-bots can be seen rushing all over with food and drink. The cheering is surpassed only by the enmity between rivals. The interchange between fans is loud and nasty. I hope security is up to the challenge. A little competition is good for the sport, but this seems like something more than that."

"I agree, Gary. This is about the worst I've ever seen. All you fans at home, watch your holo-pads. Have you ever seen anger like this? I may be a woman, but I'm also an ex-athlete, and I don't remember fans this nasty before. What do you think, Gary?"

"Absolutely not, Lucy. This is, without a doubt, the most hateful and enraged crowd of fans I've ever seen."

"Screw you!"

"Your team sucks!"

"Go home!"

"Yeah, you, you son-of-a-bitch."

"This unbridled name calling has been going back and forth for a good twenty minutes. Men, and women, are caught up in this over-the-top competitive behavior. Some children are in the stands, too. Apparently, some people have no shame in exposing their kids to such abusive behavior."

"Most wear their team jerseys, or at least, their team colors. Many are painted in their team colors. Men outnumber women twenty-to-one."

"Oh my God! Look at your holo-pads, folks. The fans are attacking each other...punching and kicking. I don't know if we can legally air this brawl as it's happening. Listen to that cursing and yelling. This is the worst stadium riot I've ever witnessed. Does that guy have a baseball bat? Red, zero in on that big guy with the bat. Did you see that? That big guy in the blue T-shirt just punched that lady in the face."

"People are pushing and shoving and throwing beer bottles at each other. Fans are being thrown out of their seats and down the concrete stairs. Fans on both sides are kicking each other. This is mayhem on a massive scale. Send in the riot police. This is nuts! A brawl on this scale is unprecedented. Everywhere we look, masses of people are fighting with each other. There must be 10,000. fights going on at the same time."

"Wait a minute, folks. Do you see what I see? Norm, pan the camera over there. Something weird is happening. Fights are stopping abruptly. Like rag dolls loosened from a child's grasp, soccer fans by the thousands are flopping to the floor. They look dead. Those left standing are knee-deep in bodies. The horror of it all is almost too much to bear. They're holding their noses. There seems to be a rancid odor coming from the stands."

"Keep the cameras rolling. Look at all those screaming fans. As you can see, folks, thousands of people are fleeing the body-lined field and the body-clogged stands. This is insane! Back to you at the studio. God, what is that smell? Lucy Jones and Gary Curdy signing off."

*   *   *

"We interrupt your regular programming for this special broadcast, direct from the White House. And now, press secretary Scooter Williams."

"My fellow Americans, Good afternoon. No, let me correct that — It is not a good afternoon; it is a terrible afternoon. I'm not going to sugarcoat this report. Our world is under attack by a plague of some sort. The death count is rising as I speak."

"You may have heard, earlier today, that the President had succumbed to this vile plague. It is my sad duty to inform you that you have heard correctly. The Vice President has also died from this rampant scourge. The Speaker of the House is now in charge. Grieve, but do not panic. Whatever this is, we will uncover the cause and rid ourselves of this threat."

"Those of us left standing share the same thought: *Am I next? Are we all going to die?* Fear is growing. Stay home and keep tuned to this channel. As I said, we mustn't panic. This plague is only striking some of us. We have to wait this thing out. Rumors are spreading that this is poison gas; maybe even a dirty bomb. This is only a rumor. We suspect this is not the case. Stay tuned to this channel. We will interrupt regular programming as we learn more. Please, just to be safe, stay away from crowds and avoid physical contact with those struck down by the plague. We now return you to your regular programing."

* * *

Like an abandoned sentinel, the mag-lev train hovers alone in the mountain pass. Breathtaking rock formations dazzle in the morning sun. A few condors glide in ever-expanding circles. The blue sky is empty of all clouds. Dust devils swirl high and blow reddish sand in all directions. Even this weather doesn't deter people from roaming around outside. This is not a scheduled stop. There is nothing around but natural beauty. The red and orange highlights of the rock formations shimmer in the distant sun. The beauty of these rocks is lost on the vacationers. All on this trip are ignoring it. They're frantically calling on useless cell-watches. One lone conductor stands among them.

"People, gather around. I don't know any more than you do about why so many of us have died, overnight. Our engineer and his assistant passed away last night and my fellow conductors are all dead. For the past week, a plague of global proportions has raged all over our planet. We, at the railroad, had hoped that it was over. That's why we embarked on this trip. Apparently, we were wrong. However, whatever it is that's hit us seems to be gone now. I'll try to get the train moving."

"What is wrong with you? My husband is dead."

"Yeah, and my wife is dead. What are you going to do about it?"

"Can you call someone?"

"I knew we shouldn't have taken this train. I just knew this wasn't the time to travel. If we had stayed home, I'll bet Pa would still be alive."

"That's just crazy, honey. This train has nothing to do with Pa dying. Whatever he caught, he must have caught it before we left. Remember, there's this crazy plague happening. We thought getting out of the city would be a way to avoid it. We were wrong. I'm sorry, son."

"Conductor, would you please do something. We can't just stand around here waiting for something to happen."

"As I just said, I don't know any more than you do. No one is answering my cell. We must be in a dead zone. For now, all you men left, help me get the dead into the baggage car. Everyone is anxious to get home. I'll try to get the train moving again. Now please, all of you, get back on board and let's see if we can get out of here."

* * *

"This is Rosanne Karr of your public TV station, reporting on something evil in our midst. It's being called a plague and it hasn't meekly tiptoed in, seeking permission to enter. It hasn't gently knocked on our door. In truth, it's kicked the door down and roared into the room like a freight train on steroids. Its cargo is death on a massive scale."

"As you can see in this holo-footage, this plague is global. Those of us not afflicted must take note of that. However, this plague is not total. It strikes one person, but not the person standing next to them. It coldly attacks a mother, but not her child. While bringing down a young person, it skips over an elderly citizen. In short, there seems to be neither rhyme nor reason to this monster. It ignores a person with multiple health issues and lays low an athlete in top-notch physical condition. This randomness of attack makes no sense."

"Our leaders are stymied now, but we must have faith that they will uncover the source of this tragedy. Here, at J.H. Regional Medical Center, their expert staff is working around the clock to trace the origination and motivation behind this epidemic."

"We here, at public TV, are covering this event 24/7. Being commercial-free, you will miss nothing. Be brave. We will prevail. We will survive. Stay tuned. More as we get it. Thank you all. Rosanne Karr signing off."

* * *

Week 2

The sunrise is beautiful. Unfortunately, it's wasted on stagnant witnesses. Most people outside can't see it. Their eyes are either closed or blank. Dawn breaks on an asphalt battlefield. The streets are awash in corpses; both singly and in piles. A reporter and her cameraman stand on a body-ladened pier. The remains piled around are of dead longshoremen and related waterfront staff.

"Phyllis Pressman of Channel 12 News reporting — Two weeks ago we would not be reporting from here. It would just be another uneventful, happy departure of a cruise ship. Today, it is an entirely different story. What a week this has been — Our fair city has seen more death this past week than in its entire history. And now, here at our beautiful waterfront, death continues to monopolize our headlines."

"This just in — The cruise ship Chariot of the Waters has returned early; one day after leaving port. The reason? 3,000 dead passengers and 1800 dead crew...all within two days of embarking. Those still alive have kept to their cabins, except for briefly exiting to eat. Since permission to hold funerals at sea has not been approved, 4,800 bodies are piled on the deck. Needless to say, the remaining passengers and crew can't wait to reach land and leave this ship of the dead. A noxious odor emanates from all these bodies."

"Madam, can you tell us anything about this tragedy at sea?"

"Can't you see I'm crying? I'm sorry. I can't say anything. My husband is one of the victims." She kneels and hugs her crying children.

"You sir, what can you tell us about this event?"

"If there ever was a voyage of the damned, this is it. The day after we left port, people started dropping like flies. It was terrible. My wife succumbed to whatever this insane disease is. Please, no more questions."

He turns his back to the camera; his shoulders shake as he holds a handkerchief to his nose.

"The Drone-cam pans the deck, from bow to stern. People are slowly wandering, as if in a trance. They seem lost. In ones and twos, they look at a corpse and whisper and cry. Cruise-bots stand by with nothing to do. It's not a pretty sight. Well, there you have it, folks...the cruise from hell. Chariot of the Waters has become Coffin of the Waters. More information as we get it. Phyllis Pressman for Channel 12 news, signing off."

"Let me digress here, for a moment. We live in a world that keeps us relatively safe. It is the least we can expect. This plague seems to defy all logic and all attempts to quell it. I feel the need to blame someone, but I don't know who. Perhaps you feel the same frustration. I would like to offer all of you out there hope for a better day, but I suspect that that is not in my power. Please don't give up and please don't panic. We will come through this.

"Thank you. Phyllis Pressman for Channel 12 News."

* * *

"This is Wade Teeter at the Masters. We have decided to continue with our classic tournament in spite of the global plague. We need a break from all this terror stalking our land. It's a beautiful day here. The sun is out and no wind at all. Chip McFarland has been shooting under par all week. This is his year for the "Green Jacket." No one else is even close to him. The weather continues to be accommodating. The crowd is properly hushed. Caddie-bots are silent and immobile. Even the birds seem to be holding their breath. This putt will not only clinch the title for Chip, it will likely put him in the record books. All eyes are on him and his 16-foot putt."

"He kneels and lines up his putt. Wait a minute, folks. Chip is swaying back and forth. He drops his putter and topples over. What the heck? His caddie has also collapsed. The crowd is moving and murmuring. Now they're shouting. People are running and falling. This is insane."

"Can you folks at home see what's happening? Mobs of people are crashing into each other and those left standing are scattered all over the course. They are screaming and weeping. There are numerous bodies left in the crowd's wake. A rancid odor is creeping from the crowd. This is crazy! Our planned escape from the plague has failed. The plague has found us. Wade Teeter signing off."

*   *   *

"Michelle Baker here for *Online Today — The Baker Blog*. I just happen to be on vacation here at Red's Hotel and Casino. Bells just started ringing. I followed them and, as you can see from my handy-cam, someone has hit a jackpot. People are coming together around the winning couple and screaming support. Crowds are gathering. Someone has hit the progressive in the slot section of the casino. The cheering is getting louder."

"Regardless of what's happening in the outside world, here in the casino is another world. Nothing else matters and there is no time. For those of you not familiar with casinos, you could find a big win before you'd find a clock. As far as seating goes, unless you're at a card table or a slot machine, there are no seats to be had."

"A young couple is embracing and jumping up and down. Music is coming from a slot machine with five sevens across the window.

The crowd is growing. This progressive hasn't been hit in six years. It's worth three million dollars."

"A casino employee stops the couple to ask some questions. He examines the machine to determine the validity of the win. He declares it legitimate. The crowd cheers. The jubilant couple agrees to pay the taxes now and take the rest of their winnings home."

"Hi. I'm Michelle Baker from *Online Today*. Tell us about your win."

"My name's Curt and this beautiful woman is Judy, my bride. We're here from Des Moines on our honeymoon. This is unbelievable! We've never won at a casino before. Does this mean we're gonna be on the internet?"

"That's exactly what it means. Prepare to be famous. What will you do with your winnings?"

"Well, we've just been offered a suite in this hotel. We're gonna take advantage of the offer and extend our honeymoon. Judy's already on her cell, telling our folks of the win. After that, I don't know. But, I want to take this opportunity to thank Red's Casino. Thank you, Thank you. Thank you."

"Judy, what do you have to say about your big win?"

"Hold on, mom, I'm talking with a reporter. I'll call you back. I'm just speechless. I don't know what to say, except thank you to the Casino. You've made us very happy. This makes our honeymoon more spectacular than we could ever have imagined."

"Michelle Baker here from Online Today, signing off."

"The crowd cheers. The bells and music keep playing. They resound throughout the casino. More people are coming. This win is special and everybody knows it. Casino-bots can be seen carrying drinks, moving chairs and emptying ashtrays."

"Wait a minute. Michelle Baker here, again. Something weird is going on. People appear to be fainting. The cheering has transformed into screaming and crying. The look of horror is spreading. The winning couple is holding onto each other. A foul odor is spreading through the casino. People are falling down or lying against their slot machines. People have jumped away from the table games and are rushing away in horror. The joy is gone...replaced by fear. Could this be a replay of Legionnaires Disease from 1976 in Philadelphia? Or, has the plague found us? I'll keep recording as long as I can. Live, here at Red's casino, Michelle Baker signing off."

*   *   *

"Wendy Blaine reporting from Mortonsville Regional Hospital. I'm here with Janet Sims, the hospital director. Doctor Sims, what is going on and how is the hospital handling it?"

"I only have a few minutes to talk to you, but here is where we are now—Since last week, our hospital has been swamped with dead bodies; all with the same symptoms. People of all ages seem to have been afflicted with an infection of some sort that causes instant death, followed by the smell of a decomposing corpse. We've never seen anything like this, nor are we prepared to handle so many cadavers at the same time. We can only hope that someone, somewhere comes up with an explanation and a cure quickly. Now, please, I have a hospital to run."

"Doctor Sims, Surgeons in O.R.-1 and O.R.-2" have collapsed. We had to pull them out and leave them in the hallway. We're trying to finish their operations now. Hurry, dozens of our staff are lying on the floors in all the hallways."

"This unprecedented situation is not just local. Our affiliates all over the nation are reporting similar situations. Not only are we flooded with terminally ill patients; now our physicians and other hospital staff are afflicted, too. If you can't turn to your local hospital in times like this, who can you turn to? Where do we go for answers? Wendy Blaine reporting for Channel 11 News, signing off."

*   *   *

"As it has for millennia, the sand yields to the waves. The clouds roll by, but the happy sounds of people at play are absent. No cheering, no yelling, no music and, most depressing, no laughing. This beachfront amusement park is as lifeless and breathless as the hundreds of corpses scattered on the rides and on the ground. Limp bodies slump over the rails of a Ferris wheel. There are as many dead bodies on the floor as there are in the bumper cars. Hover-chairs no longer hover and Quantum rocket-drives are silent. All rides are still."

"Some smaller bodies, probably of children, can be seen. Stuffed animals and fast food are everywhere. Strollers and costumes lie strewn about the grounds. The quiet is mind - numbing. Yellow tape blocks movement everywhere. A Cop-bot is on guard at each entrance to what has become a cemetery park. Park personnel wearing facemasks and hazmat suits are quietly carrying, dragging and stacking bodies near both entrances. Backhoes and bulldozers are placing masses of bodies in neat piles, later to be loaded onto trucks of all descriptions."

"Sandy Glass, a veteran reporter with twenty years on the job with Weekend News, cries as she signs off. — I don't know if I can take any more of this kind of news. This just breaks my heart. Kids, just kids. What the hell is going on? What do you want from us, God? Why children? I just can't take this anymore. The fade-to-black is more appropriate than it's ever been."

* * *

"Rusty Stokes here for Country Five Music and News. As anyone can see and hear, the fields are full and the chickens are laying. All harvesting of crops has come to a standstill. However, if you listen carefully, you can hear the cows mooing. They need to be milked. But, whether you're victim or survivor of this plague, you're not available to service these cows. Someday, we may have a Milking-bot; not today. Sadness is the biggest crop being harvested today, folks. And, if tomorrow is anything like today, we're in for a nasty week of mass death. The Grim Reaper is bringing in a bumper crop.

"It is my sad duty to report to you that our long-time engineer, Buddy Paget is dead. Buddy was a war vet and a friend of mine. Something really bad is happening. As if to mock these tragic events, the sky is blue, with a sprinkling of clouds, and the sun is shining in what appears to be a picture-perfect day."

"Reports from all over the country are sadly similar. Something evil has come for a visit. It wants us. We can only hope it doesn't want all of us. Remember, we are Americans. Our flag still waves and these colors don't run. Rusty Stokes for Country Five Music and News, signing off."

* * *

"Nat, this is Dave, again, here with an up-to-the-minute scanning of our city."

"This is Marge. Excuse the interruption, but I'm sorry to tell you that Nat has had another stroke. He's in the hospital now. We're all hoping it's just a mini-stroke, like last time. Apparently, it's not the hand of death from the plague tapping Nat on his shoulder; it's just his lousy health habits. If he wasn't in the hospital now, I swear, I'd slap some sense into him. He makes me so mad."

Marge's usually detached behavior is aflame; as vibrant as her red hair, over Nat's stroke. Although she's never told anyone outright, she's in love with Nat and has been since he hired her. She constantly worries about his health since his previous mini-stroke. She hopes that someday he will retire and finally have time for a life outside the paper; a life that will include her.

"Meanwhile, I'll be your direct link to the Chronicle. Dave, I want to make something very clear to you. Nat has a lot of faith in you. Even though you never went to journalism school, like he did, he picked you. Nat knows when someone's right for the newspaper business. His father was a reporter and his mother was an editor. He has printer's ink in his veins. Nat never married because, for him, the news business is 24/7. This paper is his family and you, Dave, are the son he never had. Remember, Nat's only 15 years older than you. He sees you as the one person in all his years of reporting to take over from him when he retires...as if he'll ever retire. You do right by him. He's counting on you...now more than ever."

"I got you, Marge. I'm so sorry. Nat's strong, though. He'll be back before you notice. Trust me. I won't let him down, and I won't let the paper down. You just keep monitoring my footage."

"Marge, what about Doc Malone. Isn't he due back from Europe now?"

"I'm sorry to be the one to tell you, Dave. Doc died yesterday, seemingly of the plague. His remains are in transit now. With Doc gone and Nat in the hospital, you and I will have to carry on for the paper, until further notice. I know it won't be easy, but we can do this. I'm sure Nat will be back soon. Get your scientific input from Sharon. Are you with me?"

Now I can't back down from this story. I have to do it for Nat, if not for myself. I promise you, Nat, unless the plague gets me, I will continue reporting on this momentous event. I owe it to you, to Sharon, to Doc, to my loyal readers, to Blake and, in spite of what Eric said, to myself.

"There is a war-like grotesqueness to this city. Corpses are everywhere and yet, something's weird. A war zone with this many bodies should show massive damage to the infrastructure. Except where people recently rioted here in the city, there is none. Not one building is damaged. However, the foul odor of rotting flesh is mind-numbing. No cars, no buses and no trolleys show any signs of damage. Just bodies...no damage to the physical plant whatsoever."

"As you can see, I'm wearing the now popular facemask. I'm calling everyone I can think of who might have a different slant on this tragedy. So far, nothing new. Due to the clutter of dead bodies, I'm giving up my car for my jetpack. Nat, I mean Marge, look at all this." —

"I'm really not comfortable using a Jet-Pac. My acrophobia is kicking in."

Dave, swooping and gliding at the two-story level, has an unobstructed but frightening, view of the devastation. He peers into mostly commercial, second-story properties. Looking in these windows, he sees shriveled bodies, and except for the quiet whoosh of his Jet-Pac, all is silent.

"I'm calling other morgues and hospitals. I've called my friend, Kevin, a lieutenant with the sheriff's department. My cousin Arnold, a fireman, is also on speed-dial. Everybody has the same response — 'Dead bodies everywhere, rancid odors and no destruction of property.'"

Dave's nose for a good story is twitching. Yet, this time it's with mixed feelings. Yes, it's a terrific story...the story of a lifetime. However, the antagonist here touches every one of us. No one is getting away with no connection to this plague. It's too widespread and too thorough. We all know someone struck down by it. No one is immune to the devastation left by this epidemic.

I know I can do this. Nat believes in me. Sharon believes in me. I can report this story. Nat, where are you when I need you? Hurry back. Maybe that Pulitzer I've been after my whole life is within my grasp now? I mean, who could ask for a more powerful story?

Sharon only stutters when she's frantic...like now. She's also passionate about her work...and very good at it. Sharon's right. This could be the story of the century. Strange though, for a moment I felt like that prize doesn't matter anymore. If Sharon survives and Nat comes back healthy and if I survive, I think I'm getting a new perspective on what's really important, and it's not any prize.

Everyone he calls tells the same story of healthy people showing up apparently starved to death. The more he looks into this mystery, the stranger it gets.

"Sharon, I just got off the phone with Helene at the hospital. At last count, 2,139 bodies have arrived in the same condition as those in your morgue. An endless stream of cars entering the hospital parking lot, all carrying shriveled corpses to deposit. The numbers are staggering. There's no way any hospital can handle this many corpses at once. This has gone way beyond strange. This macabre situation is downright scary. I'll call you later, when I know more."

"You be careful, Dave. I don't want to lose you to some crazy-ass plague."

*   *   *

"Marge, I'm calling this in because I want you with me in real time. Look at your view-screen. I recorded this scene, earlier, from my vid-glasses. Forensics is mystified. Emaciated bodies of formerly robust people of all ages have flooded morgues and hospitals all over. None has any obvious wounds — just anorexic corpses, by the millions, accompanied by a foul odor. So many cadavers in such a short time has them piled in the streets."

"But, and this is of primary importance — the path of this plague is selective. We are not all being chosen for speedy slaughter. Why some of us and not others? This is the question to be answered. This, and where does this come from? If we, can answer these two mysteries, we've got a complete story."

*   *   *

"Dave, I'm on it as we speak. Bye-the-way, Nat just walked in to the office."

"I knew it! I knew it. Hey, Nat. Welcome back. You had us worried. Don't do that again."

"Come here, you big lug. Give me a hug...and don't you try to lift me off the floor as usual."

"Yes Marge. Here's my gentlest hug. It seems to have been another mini-stroke. I don't see any side effects for now. It's good to be back. As soon as this crisis is over, I promise, I'll lose weight and eat better."

"You'd better, or I'll slap you silly. You scared us, Nat."

"Yes Marge, I promise. Now, what's the latest with Dave?"

"Dave is right here, Nat. He's sending us footage as we speak."

"Nat! Welcome back.

"Dave, Nat and I will continue monitoring major cities around the country. They all look like battlefields, with bodies on sidewalks, in the streets and in cars. From a distance, it looks like a flood of dolls and mannequins have been strewn around a child's play-town. Up close, you get the full impact of skeleton-like, decomposing corpses. This is countrywide, and growing. Keep investigating and keep us informed. I'll hold off going to press until I receive your final report."

"Again, welcome back, Nat. Don't you dare get excited, you hear me? Stay well. We need you. I need you."

Dave, ever the history buff, remembers this native-American saying: "They fell like grass before the sickle." – (the Lakota Indians, December 29, 1890, at Wounded Knee).

"On closer scrutiny, I have to say again, it's clear that no damage has been done to the infrastructure. Everything not human is being spared. Trash-bots are clearing the sidewalks of bodies. Animals and birds seem to be immune to the plague. Very strange indeed. And, the fact that not all of us in the area are infected implies that whatever this plague is, it's not poison gas. Not only is it not airborne, it seems to want some of us, but not all of us. There's something here; a pattern that we're missing."

*   *   *

"Ben Heck here for Talk Radio. My friends, we have been attacked. We are at war. We must protect ourselves. I promise you, whoever is responsible for this most foul affliction on our country will be hunted down and brought to justice. There may be evidence that China is behind this, or the Russians. If they are, we will attack and destroy them. We will spare no expense in the pursuit of these most vicious thugs. We have long memories and we do not always forgive. Stand tall, my fellow Americans. We will never surrender to this evil in our midst. We will defeat it. Thank you and stay tuned. Ben Heck of the Heck Report signing off for now."

*   *   *

Week 3

"This is Mitch Andrews of WFYI in New York," blares the holo-pad. "For three weeks, hospitals all around the country have been reporting a glut of dead bodies; all seemingly starved to death. The deaths are quick and immediately accompanied by a most foul odor. Why some of us are being struck down and others not is still a mystery."

"The White House reports that this most vicious of plagues has struck down many members of Congress. Our armed forces have been equally decimated. Troops all over the world report great numbers of casualties. The D.C. cops report thousands of dead in their ranks. It is only due to the recent increase in the use of Cop-bots that we continue to have uniformity in protecting our society."

"It is my unhappy detail to report to you of the deaths of the Speaker of the House, the President of the Senate, the Secretary of State, and the Secretary of the Treasury. This brings the line of succession to the Secretary of Defense. You can see her being given the Oath of Office on Air Force One."

"From the BBC, an epidemic of skeletal-like bodies has appeared throughout the British Isles. The Prime Minister has succumbed to the plague and, there being no line of succession in Great Britain, The Conservative Party, being the majority, has chosen a new PM. However, half of the Conservative party and half of the Labour party have been victims of the plague as well."

"Reports from the Middle East, Asia, Australia, and China concur. Last night, World News stated that this grotesque phenomenon is global. Not a country has been spared. Politicians and world leaders have fallen to the plague in the past three weeks. Governments are in turmoil. As quickly as new chosen heads of state are proposed, they fall victim to it as well. Those in high positions in government and industry are now hesitant to move up in power. They are wary of advancement at this time. The facts, such as they are, do not support a connection between one's fame or fortune and selection by the plague. If anything, observation shows the plague to be random. Time will tell."

"Tourists on holiday throughout the world have been cutting their vacations short and flocking to airports to rush home. However, those who lost loved ones while on vacation have the added burden of transporting their remains home. Bodies continue to accumulate in cities, suburbs and rural areas. Horrific doesn't even begin to describe the situation. The numbers are mind-boggling. Fatalities are estimated to be in the hundreds of millions."

"Whether it's for business or pleasure, nobody wants to be on-the-road in any way, shape or form. Travel by plane, train, bus and car is down to a minimum. And as for cruises, forget it. How can you take a cruise with the world falling down around you? The crews of our mighty fleets are unable or unwilling to set out to sea. And, who can blame them?"

"The only travel option still operating today, is a spaceship to the Moon or Mars. Those few, hearty, wealthy adventurers, who feel Space maybe safer than Earth, are still flying to the Moon and beyond. It has yet to be proven that escape to space offers safety from this plague. I'll update you as the numbers come in."

"Food production, transportation and distribution are still required and always active. No matter what is happening, we have to eat. Super markets and restaurants continue to serve us in spite of the plague."

*   *   *

"Nat, I have a confession to make. Perhaps it's a confession we all have to make. It's 2040 AD, and I'm here, in the ghetto, reporting on the plague with a twist. Except for our usual reporting on the ghetto and its statistical violence, it's now different. Let me explain"—

"Prior to the arrival of the plague, people here have had to deal with crime, 24/7. We, who don't live here, deal with crime on an occasional basis. Ghetto dwellers deal with crime and violence on a daily, and even hourly basis. The impact of this plague on the ghetto is not the same here as outside the ghetto. With homegrown violence the norm here, this plague is dealing a fatal blow to the most violent and angriest of the locals. For the first time in memory, the perpetrators of violence have become the victims. The non-violent residents here are feeling liberated. This piece of information is important. It may shed some light on the cause of the plague. Around here, they are fast welcoming the plague as a godsend."

"The gentle folk here are now free to inhabit their own streets. They feel safe for the first time in anyone's memory. They know who's being stricken by this plague, and it's not them. It's the violent members of this neighborhood. Although promised by local politicians at each election time; to cleanse the neighborhood of its unrelenting violence, heretofore these promises proved to be empty. Now, with the arrival of this plague, the ghettos are being cleaned up with no help from the authorities."

"With wars of all kinds and sizes stopped 'dead' in their tracks, peace and freedom have arrived in the ghetto. The violent have been victimized by the more violent, and all this without firing a shot. The white flag of peace is being flown here. The permanently victimized and disenfranchised welcome and cheer this plague. This should put what's happening in perspective for the rest of us."

* * *

Week 4

By the fourth week it is confirmed that casualties, worldwide, are in the billions. Vid-cams pan across body-strewn streets and sidewalks, as newscasters in all parts of the globe clamor for more airtime. They all tell the same sad story. People are frightened. They're spending as little time as possible outdoors.

* * *

The secondary road leading to the mountain campgrounds is littered with all kinds of debris. Weekend warriors and serious escapists have taken to the high country, by the tens of thousands. Most are late-comers to the inevitability of a holocaust. Many, however, are hard-core survivalists.

"Sukie, you and Trent open the storage shed and open the water valves. Dad and I will activate the wind generator and open the extra solar panels. Dannie, you and Greg start unloading the food-stuffs. John, if you secure the weapons and ammo, I'll get the kids and the dog into the compound."

"Okay, kids, listen up. This is the real thing. Something terrible has invaded our country. Although we don't know for sure what it is, this is the kind of thing we have been preparing for since you were born. Whatever this disaster is, we will survive it. Your mother and I have stocked this cabin with enough food, water and energy for at least six months."

"I want somebody on the vid-cam twenty-four/seven. We have to know what's happening outside. Other than that, no contact with anyone. Do you understand? — no talk, no text, no vid with friends. As far as anyone knows, we are away...and unreachable. I signed off from work for an early summer vacation and your mother called your schools to alert them that you would be gone, indefinitely. Now, stow your gear in your rooms and let's meet in an hour, in the great room."

"I don't want to be here. I don't want the world to be like this. Fix it! You're the dad. You're supposed to fix things."

"I can't fix this. I don't even know what this is. We just have to be here and be patient. That's why we have to monitor the radio and internet. Understand?"

"Okay dad. We'll be here and do what you say, but, this sucks. We're here and all our friends are back home. This is stupid. And, why are you so angry? We didn't make this thing that's hurting the world."

"If you're done being selfish and childish, go do your chores and I'll see you at dinner. Damn kids! You have no idea how much your mother and I do for you. No idea."

* * *

Two hours later, the family meets in the great room. Everybody is present, except dad.

"Well, this is great. We're all here and Dad's not. He's supposed to be in charge. Somebody go find him. Sukie and Trent, look outside. Everybody else, look in the cabin and be back here in ten minutes."

"Aaaaaaa!! I found Dad. He's in the shed and he's dead! And, he stinks! I mean it. He smells like nothing I ever smelled. He looks all burnt up too. I only know it's him because of his clothes. Mom, what's happening? We're supposed to be away and safe. What's wrong? If you don't stop crying, we're all gonna start crying."

Sure enough, Dad's shriveled remains are on the shed floor and the shed itself is filled with a noxious odor. At least the rest of Dad's family may just survive.

* * *

Dave Miller continues to report on the ongoing crisis — "As our News-drones reveal, the streets of our most populous cities are lined with bodies, everywhere. Endless mounds of gaunt corpses are stacked like firewood. And the stench is unbearable."

"The only comparable historical event to compare to this is The Black Death of the 14th century. It killed 75 million people (30-60% of Europe's population). However, let's not forget, that tragedy happened over a period of seven years. This is so much worse. This hideous pandemic has killed more people in the past three weeks than all the wars fought throughout history, combined. Nothing on this scale has ever been recorded."

"About the only positive effect of the plague is that the current "hot" wars in the Middle East, Russia and North Korea have all come to a sudden halt. The worldwide Islamist Jihad has also come to an abrupt end. The battlefields in all these regions are littered with bodies; on both sides. More than half the standing armies of all parties are gone; struck down in mid-sentence by some hidden force. No side wants to fight when more than half their troops are dying from an unseen enemy."

"Additionally, the angriest of warriors, those who led these armies are themselves, being decimated by this plague. There are no surviving warlords and generals to lead these conflicts. No ethnic wars, no religious wars, no wars of disputed territories; no wars, period. This might be the end to all wars. One can only hope. So far, this is the singular bit of good news since the plague's arrival."

"Even the 'Border Wars' that have raged since the beginning of this century are, for the first time, at a standstill. Sixty-percent of our Border Patrol officers have been stricken. The number of illegal immigrants desperate to cross our borders has been cut in half; because of this plague. No one in this part of the country knows what to do. There's an eerie cease-fire along the border with Mexico, from Texas to California."

* * *

"As you can see, our light-rail line is at a standstill. Nothing is going anywhere. They just sit, silently, with a cargo of corpses scattered in the seats and on the floor. Except for brief forays for food, the streets are empty of healthy people. Although all our news services have reported that the plague is not airborne, people act as though it is. They stay home as much as possible, and when out, wear their face masks and do their best to avoid groups."

"Our zoos are still open to the public. If not for volunteers from all animal rescue organizations, our zoo population would be devastated. People, especially families, are returning to non-technological forms of entertainment and enjoyment. Museums and galleries and parks are again popular gathering places. I think people just want be with others in times of peril...as long as they believe this plague is not catching."

* * *

"Richard Wallace reporting from the Middle East. A most amazing, unusual atmosphere here. For the first time in years, there's no sound. A surreal quiet blankets the countryside and the city. No rockets. No gunfire. No ambulance sirens. No people yelling in the streets. Terrorism has hit a blank wall. The only sound is the isolated wailing of a survivor."

"This entire area is a ghost town. Corpses are everywhere, but live people are strangely absent. People, fearing that this epidemic is airborne, are staying indoors. Wind, dust and a few predator birds are all that's moving. The dust is quickly covering many of the carcasses. The Trash-bots have emerged and are busy sweeping the corpses and sand into neat piles for pickup. The quiet is equal to the carnage. I've never seen anything like this. No more war...at least for now. Just deadly quiet and swirling sand."

"Fear is the winner here. Terror and despair have overcome every other player on this stage. I've been on empty movie sets and at archeological digs, and this is just like that. No people, no sound and no movement of any kind. This is a deathly calm and a most deadly way to win peace. We can only hope it's over soon."

"Soldiers are no longer needed as war has become obsolete. No tanks, no planes and no troops. It's the strangest situation. In the midst of mass death, there is no war. Richard Wallace signing off."

*   *   *

"Sam Reid here, from Channel 14 News. I'm at an auto assembly plant in the heartland. As you can see, no work is being done today. Even though all buildings are now fully automated, all machines are stopped. As with other businesses, masses of corpses have been hastily removed or stored out of sight. Yet, while the plague, or whatever it is, rages, people are staying home just in case this thing is airborne. It is strange, indeed, to see this 2 ½-million square-foot plant silent. No human activity and no robot activity."

"This just in — Several of our carriers and battle ships at sea are requesting orders for further movement. They don't know whether to stay at sea or to return to port. Their crew members have suffered a thirty-five percent loss of life. All they know is that they've been ordered not to hold burials at sea until further notice."

"Back here, many movie theaters have become temporary morgues. A third of their patrons from the past three weeks lie in seats or on the floors. We, who have survived, don't know what to do. Many of our office buildings, stadiums, colleges, buses, trucks of all sizes, highways, playgrounds, bars, parks, and all manner of gathering places, have all become holding pens for corpses. We can't go on like this much longer. Sam Reid, Channel 14 News, signing off."

"Hold it. This just in from our news headquarters — The Secretary of Defense has fallen victim to the plague, as has the Attorney General. For the first time in the history of our nation, the line of succession has made it to the Secretary of the Interior. She is being given the Oath of Office as we speak. God help us all."

"The government has declared Martial law. This declaration is appropriate, but keep in mind that up to 1/3 or more of all our armed forces are dead. All our troops have been depleted. However, wars, large and small, have come to a standstill. Those troops are on their way home as we speak. Who do you fight first...your sworn enemy or the plague? The troops still alive are the ones who have to stack and store the 1/3 who have succumbed to the plague. That doesn't leave too many healthy troops for a deployment of any kind."

* * *

"Carson Morrow for Channel 10 News, reporting from P.S.U. in Philadelphia. The plague's effect on college campuses has been as expected...and different. Science "profs" from all disciplines have gotten together to pool their talents to try to get a handle on the plague. So far, no one has a clue as to its origin. Further, no one has any idea how to stop it."

* * *

"Most students have left for home or are keeping to their dorms. Obviously, all classes have been canceled. The few students braving the outdoors seem to be students of the physical sciences and pre-med students. Strangely enough, art majors and some

English majors are also investigating on campus. They claim to be repulsed by the numerous corpses and yet, simultaneously attracted to them, as visual images for art."

* * *

"Linda. are you making a holo-vid with your cam? You have to capture this, for all of us. You're the best and we need someone creative on this."

"You bet. I'm all over this. It's simultaneously repulsive and attractive. I'll do my best, guys."

"Hey, Michael, can you picture these bodies in paint? If only I could paint smell. I want to draw them and then digitize my drawings. Listen Jackie, I'm kind of upset with myself; I can't believe the horror of these tragic deaths and, at the same time, I want to sculpt them into some kind of memorial to the victims. They remind me of Goya's *Tragedies of War.*"

The few English majors out and about are also appropriately repulsed by these horrible deaths, and yet attracted to them as content for prose and poetry. "Harry, listen to this poem I just wrote about the plague — "

'Plague has come so silently, beware its deadly touch.

Stops at nothing, march of death; it sucks the life from much.

Young and old, no one is safe, 'cause attitude is all.

Rid yourself of anger now, or you will get the call.

To die and shrivel up to naught, in so short a time.

Not live to see new world of love, a world that is sublime.'

"I know, I know. It's terrible to be thinking of writing when all around us are dying. I can't help it. Painters paint, writers write. That's what we do."

"Randy, how do you know that anger is the cause of the plague and that a world of love is coming? Do you know something the rest of us don't?"

"I don't know where that came from. It just came out when I wrote the poem."

*   *   *

Week 5

"Ken Billings, here at MLK Jr. Middle School. Unfortunately, what we have here is a double whammy. First, the children have been exposed to death; not just death of an individual friend or favorite teacher, but death on a massive scale. These deaths of their peers and their teachers are shocking, to say the least. This has been a devastating blow for all. Second, the trauma caused by these untimely, horrible deaths is permeating the entire student body, as well as the surviving staff."

"The children are having a difficult time adjusting to the abrupt demise of some of their favorite teachers. Those who witnessed these deaths will have to live with the terrifying and grisly memories for years to come. The students who witnessed the horrifying demise of their fellow classmates have the added impact of it happening to people their own age."

"However you view it, these past four weeks have had an extraordinary impact on the youth of our world and will surely lead to long-range suffering for many. It will be a long time before adults and children can understand, accept and move on from this horrific disaster. Ken Billings for NCI News, signing off."

"In a related news story, the series of riots all over the world seems to have subsided. It looks as if all the rioters have either been incarcerated or struck down by the plague. Law and order seems to be in hands of our Cop-bots. They are programmed to keep the peace, without anger. They are efficient, but emotionless. "

* * *

"An immediate change in our society is our sporting events. Even the stadiums not being used to store cadavers are empty. People are staying home and avoiding crowds. This is not to say that sporting events would take place if people did leave their homes. With more than half of all professional sports figures, men and women, dead of the plague, there aren't any teams with a full roster left. What I'm saying is that if this murderous plague were to end tomorrow, there isn't a professional team left, of any particular sport, to stage a game. Our world has been acutely changed overnight."

* * *

"South Sudan, Syria, Iraq, Afghanistan, North Korea, Crimea, Kashmir, all drug-exporting countries, and any other 'hot-spots' of war and violence are welcoming this plague with an understated skepticism. Having known nothing but war for generations, they are wary of any new changes in their way of life, but being weary of war, they are open to almost any other option. As they mourn their dead, they celebrate the deaths of their suppressors. It is a rude reminder to those of us free of oppression and war that not all of the world has been as fortunate as we are."

* * *

Week 6

"Charlie Preacher of Channel 3 News here. The dead are piled up everywhere you look. Urban centers, suburban areas and rural locations are all the same. So many corpses in so short a time. Stadiums and athletic fields of all sizes are filling up with dead bodies. We can't store them all. Holo-evangelists of all persuasions are coming out of the woodwork claiming the 'End of Days' to be here. They say this is biblical retribution for living in sin. Some are shouting this message from street corners, others from their pulpits."

"Into this fertile bed of frozen fear have jumped preachers of every size and persuasion, with their 'good book' held high. Last night, the first night of cleared streets in our towns and cities, led to a profusion of candlelight vigils. These were led by big-city holo-evangelists and their small-town wannabes. They were all properly somber, with an 'Elmer Gantry' sprinkling of fire and brimstone preaching. They beat their drums of faith with a fervor reserved for apocalyptic events. Sin, damnation and redemption were all spotlighted."

"The next day, rallies, small and large, were held around the country. Some rallies overflowed into the streets and became massive parades of those caught up in religious fury. Righteous indignation poured from these riders of the pulpit. They are convinced that God is behind this plague and we, his children, are the targets of his anger."

"Candlelight vigils are being held countrywide. The mood is somber and dismal. People weeping and praying are commonplace. The marches go nowhere. When you think about it, where can you go? Where should you go? Fear is everywhere. Fear rules."

"As the congregations of frightened followers grows to epic proportions, religious filibusters of all persuasions spew forth a continuous flow of dire predictions. Over and over, these preachers are claiming that this plague is just one more sign of the End of Days. They call on us to focus on the reemergence of Israel since 1948, the chaos in the Middle East and the rise of the Islamic State, the ubiquitous increase of all sorts of immorality and the spread of the Christian gospel. They say all this is paving the way for The Second Coming of Jesus. And yet, all this, in spite of the fact that Islam is now the most popular religion in the world."

"Add to these horrible predictions events such as global warming, the extinction of tens of thousands of species and epidemics like Aids and Ebola, and these predictions can't easily be dismissed. When you think about it, who can argue with them? Who knows the true nature of the plague? Perhaps our religious texts are truly prophetic? What if they're right? What do we do? How do we stop this?"

"Rich and poor, black and white, old and young, male and female, believer and atheist — none of these distinctions mean anything anymore. If the plague wants you, it gets you. The fact that no country has been spared by this plague suggests that no government can be singled out as the culprit. We are all in this together. There are no winners. 'The enemy of my enemy is my friend.' And, never forget, the enemy here is the plague."

* * *

"The White House has ordered us to refrain from burying bodies. We can't continue like this much longer. Maybe the dead are the lucky ones. We who survive know what hell looks like. It brings to mind the 16th century paintings of Hieronymus Bosch. We see it everywhere. Back to the studio."

"Hold on, Charlie. Pardon the pun, but we have drone-footage of a prison riot stopped dead in its tracks two days ago. The penitentiary at Francis Falls was at a standoff with the guards and local police when this plague hit. Three hundred prisoners and thirty-six of our city's finest fell in Day One. The plague brought this riot to an unexpected halt. The remaining prisoners, while not in lockup, continue to occupy the prison compound. I don't think they'd leave if given the opportunity. They seem shell-shocked. They've stacked the bodies of those lost to this invader in the yard and are, for the most part, quiet. They seem as bewildered as the rest of us. Charlie Preacher for Channel 3 News signing off for now."

*   *   *

Dave records on his vid-cam: "By the end of Week Six, an unmistakable, bizarre pattern has become quite clear —To everybody's surprise, the weakest and gentlest among us seem to be the least susceptible to the fatal affliction. To everyone's astonishment, the strong, the violent, the tough, and the angry are succumbing to it. Painlessly, they just stop eating. They quickly lose weight and the will to live. They simply lay down, shrivel up and die."

"The big and the strong will be laid low; the soft and the tender will be lifted up." Dave's history class on Lao Tzu.

"Prayer can't stop it. Those lost in the grip of fear and rage, perish. Nothing works...with one exception. The only angry people to survive are those who give up their former attitude. It has become crystal clear that anger is the culprit. The more you're fear-based and angry, the quicker your demise. The more peaceful and loving you are, the better your chances for survival. Those who refuse to change, get angrier, which, in the long run only hastens their departure from this world."

"Apparently, the ghetto dwellers knew, or suspected, long before the rest of us. They sensed that anger was the cause of this plague. They saw the gang-bangers die in great numbers. They knew who the toughest, angriest members of their neighborhoods were. They also knew who the survivors were — the gentlest of folk. They saw the unconditional love preached in their churches finally conquering the mighty; the angry. They were the first to recognize that, mercilessly, the meek were inheriting the earth. They knew the words of the 'good book'. It's no wonder they rejoiced at this plague."

"What an odd scene we have. As you can see, in their final act of denial, the last of our angry brothers and sisters are cursing their situation and raising their collective fists to the heavens in a rampage of furor. Then they collapse and die."

* * *

"Dave, I'm calling you because I've made some progress in my lab. After examining tissue, bone and brain matter, I'm convinced that, as you said, this plague is neither airborne nor viral. I'm also quite certain that it didn't arrive here on some meteorite or bubble up from deep in the Earth."

"All that having been said, I do see a pattern of symptoms that suggest the answer to the plague's origin and possibly its cure, is to be found in neuroscience."

"What does that mean, Sharon? Are you saying the brain has something to do with this?"

"That's exactly what I'm saying, Dave. I know, it sounds a little crazy, but hear me out. For years now, Dr. Robert Lanza, PhD., has been promoting the idea that all of the material world is created by the mind. Although he's not the only one to have this mindset, he's as good as any representative of this new paradigm in science. Look, we now know that the common denominator in these plague deaths is anger. We also know that anger comes from fear. Further, we know that the complement of fear is love; unconditional love."

"Are you with me so far?"

"Yes, I'm following you. Please, tell me more."

"The only people to be threatened by the plague and to have survived it are those who changed their outlook from one of fear to one of love."

"You're beginning to sound like Gandhi. He said: 'Become the change you wish to see.'"

"Well, here is where it gets real interesting. I've isolated some brain matter linked to neurotransmitters and added some chemicals and come up with a cocktail I think can help those on the brink of transforming their demeanor from one of fear to one of love. I am calling this concoction Vitriol-7. There's no time for clinical trials. I, we, have to act fast. Use your connections at the Chronicle and with other media to get the news of this cure out

ASAP. We need to make this drug available to all who can be helped by it."

"Sharon, are you saying you can chemically eliminate fear and anger from a person?"

"No, Dave, that's not what I'm saying. I don't have time here to give you a crash course in neuroscience or Dr. Lanza's 'Bio-Centrism'. What I can tell you is that once you accept that we don't find the world as it is, but as we make it, you open the door to a whole new understanding of the universe and how it operates."

"The scientific conflict between Idealism and Materialism seems to be weighing in heavily in favor of Idealism. In other words — matter does not create mind; mind creates matter. This opens the door, wider, to Quantum Mechanics."

"You should know from your Zen studies that the way out of fear and anger is not to eliminate them but to transcend them. I remember my studies in Eastern philosophy and how Buddhism encourages the elimination of what they call 'the three poisons – Greed, Anger and Ignorance'. They are part of the human equation and always will be. Transcendence leads to inner peace. By turning within, the course of all meditation, you end suffering and achieve inner peace."

"However, many people cannot accomplish this by pure meditation. Maybe they haven't got the temperament or even the time. My med, 'Vitriol-7,' suppresses the anger chemically, thereby giving the individual the chance to overcome their anger, take charge of it and move beyond it. Do you understand what I'm saying? I need you to get this right because you are the one to get the word out on this. You are the media."

"I'll do my best, dear. I don't profess to understand all that you've said here, but I believe in you. If you say you have a possible cure, I'm ready to run with it. Keep working. I'll get back to you soon. I love you. Bye."

*   *   *

"Dave Miller reporting. By the time the cause of the plague was thoroughly understood, it was too late to do anything about it. The only exceptions were those who received the *'Miller-Cure'*. Six weeks after it began, the plague stopped. All the angry people in the world were dead. The meek had mercilessly inherited the Earth. What a bizarre, mixed-blessing, turn of events. Peace and love are now free to reign on a global scale. May God have mercy on the souls of our dear departed."

*   *   *

Dave remembers reading: *"You will not be punished for your anger. You will be punished by your anger."*— Confucius, 2,500 BC. He continues —

"The pandemic began six weeks ago. This plague has run rampant, ravaging the human population of planet Earth. We know when it began, and now we know what caused it. We who have survived it are grateful that it has stopped. It's been quick. It's been quiet. It's been thorough. The strong, the mighty, well-armed or not, have followed a terminal, downhill slide. They never saw it coming. What acted like a plague has proven itself to be neither air-borne nor viral."

"Apparently, a 'tipping-point', in this case, three billion individuals, was reached. That number of three billion angry persons, out of nine billion total population, caused the plague. No other factor seems to matter. When one out of every three people is angry, the world is so infected by this anger that a plague of global proportions is born. It would seem that Michael Jackson was correct when he sang, 'We are the world.'"

"At last count, three billion people have perished. However, Dr. Sharon Miller's cure, Vitriol-7, has saved one-tenth of one percent of the three billion victims. This may not seem like much, but it comes to three million lives saved. I think she deserves the Nobel Prize in Medicine for this year."

"And then, just as mysteriously as it began, it stopped. Apparently, it reached its required number of deaths to halt. It has now been twenty-four hours with no new deaths reported. We can only hope that this is a sign that the plague has ended. We were nine billion people just six weeks ago, and now we are six billion. What a massive loss of life."

"We who have survived are stunned...by the loss of so many of our brethren and by our very survival. Why now? Why us? What does all this mean? What is the message here?"

*   *   *

"Scooter Williams here at the White House, for an update — Our newly-sworn in President, Diana Planter, former head of the Department of the Interior, and Congress, have issued this joint statement as part of the enactment of Martial law. We can't allow the continued dumping of bodies in the oceans or the burying of them in the deserts. This will pollute our environment."

"Consequently, both houses of Congress have unanimously enacted a new, two-percent tax. The revenue from this tax will go to pay for our portion of the cremations of three billion victims of the Plague. Other countries are doing the same. This must be done quickly and efficiently or we could have a new crisis on our hands... rotting carcasses are a breeding ground for disease. Place your dead outside; on the sidewalk or lawn. Trucks will come around to pick them up. This is the only way we're going to save the rest of us from illness or death. Stay tuned for more details. Scooter Williams signing off, direct from the White House, and may God have mercy on their souls."

* * *

"Fear, having had more than its day in court, has ruled Earth for hundreds of thousands of years. Now, for the first time in history, love has replaced it. Fear is out and love is in. Anger is dead. May it rest in peace. Now what? What will the remaining world's population do? Cars have started sporting bumper stickers that read: ANGER KILLS/LOVE LIVES. T-shirts have appeared with the phrases: LOVE TRUMPS ANGER and ANGER IS NOT YOUR FRIEND."

* * *

Dave, pale and slender, and Sharon, his tall, attractive wife, sit at their kitchen table, reviewing events of the past six weeks —

"I know you've always had a fear of missing something important in your work, but that isn't the case this time. Once we ruled out every possible medical reason for the plague, we could more clearly see the pattern surrounding it. Once you knew the cause was psychological, you let your science run wild in your search for a cure."

"By the way, this hot chocolate is delicious. I don't know how you people can drink coffee. I don't care for the smell or the taste; never have."

"I don't think I could have gotten through med school without coffee. Now, back to the issue at hand. Anger, as the underlying cause behind the plague, is apparent now. When enough angry people were alive, at the same time, the population of the earth reached a tipping point...and the plague was born."

"You know challenges and me. Once I get my mind set on solving something, I don't give up. I really wanted to find a cure for the plague. Although, by the time I came up with Vitriol-7, I was too late to help most of the three billion victims. But, I'll settle for the three million lives saved by the drug."

"I can't believe I'm saying this. We now know the real origin of the plague, and it is us. We are the world. I know this isn't classical science, and I hate to use the word "spiritual", but there's no other word I can think of right now. Maybe 'Idealism', which has been triumphing over 'Materialism' lately is a better term. However, whichever way you look at it, we can no longer claim to be helpless victims. We are responsible for the world in which we live. We can't blame this plague...or anything else on outside forces exclusively."

"In a way, we've been dragged, kicking and screaming, to a second chance; a chance to get it right. We are not choosing to follow a path without anger; it's being forced on us. We who have survived this plague will now live in a world without anger...whether we like it or not. If it works, great. If not, I don't know what we'll do. We've spent the last 20,000 years living with anger. I'm up for trying a world without it."

"Remember, a world without anger is a world without fear, and a world without fear can be a world directed by unconditional love. Isn't this the world we were promised 2,000 years ago, by

Jesus? Or, 2,500 years ago, if you're a Buddhist. This is so unscientific, it scares me."

"God, I'm not comfortable with this new approach to science. You see, I'm already using the term, "God". It just doesn't feel scientific. At times, it smacks not of physics, but of metaphysics. Who knew, or even suspected, six weeks ago that a psychological condition, like anger, would prove to be the culprit? On one thing we can agree, though — we couldn't be more relieved and happy that it's over. You know, according to 'Idealism', this is our gift to ourselves. This just gets stranger and stranger."

"I know what you mean, Sharon. I have a confession to make. I used to wonder if I was being too objective in my reporting. How do you relate to people you only know peripherally? Can you? I know I can empathize with those with whom I'm on intimate terms. I used to feel so detached. I know where that comes from. I mean, I've been studying Eastern philosophy for half my life. Zen teaches detachment. I'm not aloof. I don't want people to suffer. I just don't seem to fall apart at tragic news the way I'm supposed to...the way other people do. All I'm saying is that I wondered, for a long time, if I cared enough about the people I reported on."

"I remember in my high school history class our studies included the assassination of President John F. Kennedy. I gasped when I first read that he was shot. I didn't know him. I never met him. Yet, I cared. I was glad that I cared; that I felt something. But, that was a long time ago. Can I still care? I think so. I hope so. I don't want to just write about what happens to people. I want to care about what happens to them, too."

"Perhaps that's what makes for good journalism. I have no agenda but the truth. I have to be able to see the big picture. I have to be able to report the *who, what, why, when, and where* of a story.

I need to focus on facts. I suppose I could have been a detective. Then again, I'm not just a reporter; I'm an investigative reporter. Perhaps it just goes with the territory. Either way, with Blake gone, I have to accept my new position and be prepared for its consequences and rewards."

* * *

"I've got to take this call Sharon. It's from my ex-wife, Jill. Hi Jill, what's this call about? Oh, no! Oh, Jill, I'm so sorry. What can I do? I'll be there as soon as I can. 'Bye."

"What was that all about, Dave? Are you crying? Dave, what is it?"

"That call was from my Jill. Our son, Brad is dead; a victim of the plague. I'm so sorry. He never forgave me for my divorce from Jill. He's been angry since I left home...his home."

"Dave, there was nothing you could have done. Jill demanded that you leave. She served you divorce papers."

"Yeah, I know. Still, try explaining that to a fifteen-year-old. He's hated me since I left. And now he's gone and I'll never be able to patch things up with him. Dammit! It's not fair. He was one of the most tortured souls I know. He's gone and I can't do a thing about it. I really let him down. I feel terrible."

Sharon embraces a shaking, crying Dave.

"Dave, don't you go tearing yourself down. Since we've been together, you've tried numerous times to reach out to Brad. He just wouldn't meet you half way. You're not a bad person. Go comfort Jill, but don't blame yourself."

*   *   *

"Jill, I'm so sorry. I know Brad and I had a strained relationship, but I loved him. I just couldn't get through to him."

"You're not getting off that easy, Dave. You killed Brad the day you cheated on me. Your infidelity cost us our marriage and sent Brad into a depression he never recovered from. He was already dead when the plague got him."

"Jill, not a day goes by that I don't think of Brad and what I did to both of you. I would give my life if I could take it back, but I can't. I did a stupid, selfish thing and caused irreparable harm…to you, to Brad and, even though you don't believe it, to myself."

"I learned my lesson the hard way. I've never done anything like that again."

"It's nice to hear, Dave, but little comfort. Late for me and way too late for Brad. I don't know what to think anymore. If you've come here for forgiveness, I think you've come to the wrong place. Please, just go. There's nothing you can say or do that will change anything at this point."

With tears in his eyes and a huge sadness having taken over his heart, Dave leaves Jill's house. His love for Sharon is about the only thing holding him together now. His devotion to Sharon and his job will have to sustain him from now on. Try as he might, he cannot change the past. He cannot undo past wrong-doings.

Perhaps I can learn from all this tragedy and sadness and become a better human being. I hope so. The price for all this is so high, it's almost unbearable. I do love Jill, I just stopped being in love with her. And, I know in my heart that I never stopped loving Brad. I just wish I could have reached him.

*   *   *

"Gwen Woodruff of Channel 3 News here, with my exclusive interview with Dr. Maureen Osborn of Yale Medical School and Dr. Peter Lazlow of the Harvard Psychology Department."

"Here they are folks. These are the two psychologists who first recognized the true, medical nature of our recent epidemic. Welcome to you both. Dr. Osborn, let's begin with you. When did you first realize that anger was a key factor in the plague?"

"As you know, Gwen, Dr. Lazlow and I have worked together before. When I realized what was happening with these corpses, I immediately called Peter, and conferred. He too, had a suspicion that the plague was neither air-borne nor viral. After weeks of examining data from all over the world, we began to see a pattern in the victims."

"There has been an abundance of athletes, like Jordan Clay, dropping dead and shriveling up, on the playing field. Sonny Davis dropping dead in the ring. Fringe preachers, like Jimmy Joe Bleaker, and some of our most decorated soldiers fell where they stood. Rogue cops who turned out to be less than clean and ruthless gang members, followed suit. Abusive mates and siblings by the hundreds of millions have died. Extremist politicians like Judy Rulani and – TV pundits like Ben Peck and movers and shakers, from all walks of life."

"Dr. Lazlow, what then?"

"Well, Gwen, being research psychologists, we checked the data several times, just to reassure ourselves that our conclusions were on solid ground. With the exception of those few 'heavy-hitters' who renounced their anger and, subsequently, survived the plague, there was no doubt in our minds that fear and its manifestation anger, was the culprit. We now had a cause for the plague, but still no way of stopping it."

"It made us think of Sherlock Holmes: *"When you have eliminated the impossible, whatever remains, however improbable, must be the truth."*

"Now that the epidemic is over, does this mean that the world will no longer live in fear? Are we to have a 'new world order' of some sort?"

"Now that the plague is over, we have to get on with how we are going to live from now on. It just can't be business as usual. We have to change. We have to grow. I suppose when you think about it, we have to evolve."

"You see, Gwen, anger is no longer an option. Not for anyone who wants to live a long life."

"What kind of a world does this promote? Dr. Osborn, will you comment, please?"

"Much of our world will be the same, but much of it will be different. How different remains to be seen."

"Can you give us an example of the 'new' world awaiting us?"

"With anger and fear out, the most likely atmosphere to prevail is its complement, love; unconditional love. This has far-reaching implications for many aspects of our culture. Prophets and sages, throughout history, have all preached the same message of love. Now, those of us who have survived the plague are getting a chance to see if they were right."

"Let's take sports, for example. Competition in sports should remain popular. Sports celebrities will still emerge from the crowd. Talent and hard work will not be denied. It's just that those who are defeated on the field won't be made to feel like losers. 'High-fiving' and 'victory-dancing' is definitely out. They did their best, but the other team won. Tomorrow is another day. When you think about it, it is a more civilized way to live."

"Dr. Lazlow" what might be different in our society as a result of this strange turn of events?"

"With anger out of the equation, violence has quickly become a thing of the past. Disputes and disagreements are being settled non-violently. With anger gone, road-rage is gone. Diplomacy and goodwill are dominating. If this keeps up, I predict that war will become a rare, if not extinct, occurrence. We always thought that our strength lay in our technology. Obviously, it does not. Our strength, our salvation, lies in our humanity— As Dr. Osborn just said, we are being forced to evolve, quickly, into better people."

"It's not only a question of having to evolve into better, more loving people. You have to remember that the angriest of us are now gone. Those of us left, even those with tendencies towards anger, are the least angry of us all. This new paradigm covers a much smaller range of emotion from anger (think fear) to love (think unconditional). Our most angry people are the least angry in our history."

"How true. Dr. Osborn, what can you add to these predictions?"

"Our court system will have to be re-evaluated and re-aligned with our new paradigm. We're unlikely to continue to have much of a 'death-row' in our prisons because our prison population is going to be much, much smaller. It's likely that fist fights and brawls will go the way of bell-bottom trousers. I think it will be awhile before we fully grasp the magnitude of this plague on our lifestyle. Who knows how much of our society has been fear-based? We're entering new territory here."

"Well folks, it appears that we're in for a new society. Perhaps greed might just be replaced by generosity. With anger gone, maybe, just maybe, the 'Golden Rule' will become the order of the day. Tune in tomorrow when my guest will be Major Theresa Gandhi of the Salvation Army. Thank you and good night. This is Gwen Woodruff of Channel 3 News signing off."

                              *   *   *

"Ken Billings here for NCI News with an update from around town and around the country. Tonight, a special report on the ongoing transformation of our society. One of the major issues coming up is — What to do about food? The fact that most of our food is now grown, hydroponically, in sanitary rooms or created in petri dishes, may still be our number one source of protein. Do you still hunt, fish and slaughter? Are Buddhists right? Will vegans prevail? Here to discuss these issues are Sheldon Kasing of the NRA and Dr. Andrew Beil of the President's Commission on Nutrition. Sheldon, let's begin with you. What changes have occurred in the NRA since the end of the plague?"

"Ken, contrary to popular expectations, not very much has changed. People still want to eat meat and fish. Anger was never a prime issue with hunters and fisherman. We target shoot and hunt game for the sport of it or to feed our families. We do not do it out of anger. In fact, with fear and anger gone, there is no longer a question of gun safety. We don't have to worry about guns falling into the wrong hands. There are no wrong hands any more. End of story."

"Dr. Beil, your response to Mr. Kasing" —

"Although Shel and I have traditionally been on opposite sides of the gun issue, he's right. That is no longer the case. Our food supply continues to be a combination of hunted, farmed and harvested food...of all types. Absent anger, people still need to eat and to have different food preferences. Our main objective at the Commission on Nutrition is still to promote the healthiest diet possible."

"Well, there you have it folks. Those of us who were carnivores before the plague continue to eat meat and those of us who were vegetarians continue as we were. Food provision remains as it was B.P. (before the plague). And, additionally, the gun lobby is now issue-free. What a nice surprise."

*   *   *

"Dave Miller, here with an update — Two months after the end of the plague, changes in our society are becoming more apparent. The offices at the Daily Chronicle are humming with commotion. Reporters and copy editors struggle to keep up with the work. Newly hired staff, to replace those lost to the plague, are either at their computers or running here and there with news updates. 'Foodie' is busy keeping the staff well-supplied with coffee and snacks."

"One of the updates is particularly significant. When you look up and down the streets outside the Chronicle office, no bodies are to be seen. The Trash-bots have been working 24/7 on this massive cleanup. The bulk pick-up of corpses has been swift and thorough. Bulldozers and backhoes have been helping the Trash-bots with the cleanup. Streets and sidewalks are open and, with a third of the population gone, less crowded. Along with the disappearance of dead bodies, went the putrid odor that accompanied them."

"Not having a body to bury or cremate locally, survivors have been issued stars to put in their windows, as has been the tradition for households of troops killed in action. Appropriate medals, not unlike Purple Hearts, are to be disseminated in the near future. Although each departed soul was a victim of his or her own anger, they were still victims of the plague. One can't help feeling sorry for them and for those they left behind. The content carried by each victim and their DNA on record, have helped identify him or her. All personal effects are being turned over to their families as quickly as possible."

"Also of note, living through a major disaster like this plague certainly puts things in perspective. Before the plague, things like awards, fame, fortune, position, status, and power were given high priority. We made them important. This horror show we've just survived makes it very clear that they were, at best, petty. Family, friends, people...life in general is more important than all these other things. Smart can be a given...at an early age. Wisdom has to be earned; over many years...and we are painfully learning it."

"Or, to put it another way — 'The most important things in life aren't things.' When humanity ignores small, understated, warnings from Mother Nature, she force-feeds us a banquet of humble pie and stimulants. She knows that when coerced to mature and evolve, we do. This plague has been one nasty, ruthless wakeup call."

"Any Zen master will tell you to be in harmony with nature and with yourself. 'Find what makes your heart sing and create your own music.' Then, as you turn within, all truths will be revealed. You don't eliminate the bad or negative qualities of life from the world; you transcend them. If you permanently eliminated negatives from the world, they're would be nothing left to transcend. The game of evolution would be over."

*   *   *

In Nat's office at the Chronicle —

"Look Boss, this has been my story from the beginning. My wife, Sharon, was one of the first persons to see a trend in the plague, and I was the first to investigate the tragedy and to write about it. It's not that I don't want to share my byline. Actually... it's exactly that. If I'm ever going to get the validation and recognition that I deserve, it's by reporting a story like this plague. I don't mean to sound uncaring or selfish, but you, of all people, should know how hard I've worked for this."

"This story is bigger than any one person, Dave. You will, of course, continue to cover the plague and its consequences on a national and global scale, but the rest of our staff will pursue influences in their respective areas of expertise. You handle the general and they'll handle the specific."

"Okay Boss, but no infringing on my territory."

I can't let anyone take over my reporting. This plague story is my ticket to the big time. No more taking second place because I never went to college. No more playing second fiddle to Sharon's top-drawer degrees and early successes. This is my time. I can feel it. Sharon and I are in this together.

"Annabelle, what's the story from Real Estate?"

"Nat, unlike what I hear about food and the NRA, the plague is having a major influence on real estate. With a third of the population gone, the need for new housing has disappeared. I don't mean that people don't need real estate anymore; it's just that the availability of existing properties is now immense. With such an increase in saleable properties, the need for new structures is way down. Resales are big. Really big."

"Before the plague, commercial and factory real estate was scarce. With climate change causing a rising of the seas and subsequent flooding of coastal cities, real estate was scarce and becoming even scarcer. Now, due to a drastic reduction in population, it's plentiful and cheap. As a result, singular real estate profits are declining. At the same time, though, real estate volume is rising exponentially. Since the plague, everyone has a *friend* in the real estate business. Employment opportunities to re-purpose properties and repair infrastructure have opened up careers in construction on a massive scale."

"In fact, Nat, with all the work needed to refurbish, restore and reconfigure existing properties, plus the huge openings for workers to restore our deteriorating infrastructure, real estate alone can probably offer us a zero-unemployment rate for the first time in our history."

"Although politicians have promised for decades to clean up ghettos and to repair our crumbling infrastructure, work in both these areas has been stalled or ignored for as long as anyone can remember. This is no longer the case. Ghettos and other unsafe neighborhoods are disappearing as we speak. Ghettos may be ugly, for the time being, but they're no longer dangerous. Broken windows are being repaired, graffiti is being cleaned up and trash of all kinds is being carted away. Habitat for Humanity has openings for hundreds of thousands of people."

"People formerly trapped in their homes are again taking over the streets. Gardens and small businesses are springing up everywhere. For the first time in years, block parties are happening. Dare I say it? Happiness and a positive attitude are the new, prevailing atmosphere in all neighborhoods. These positive changes are especially acute in our former ghettos. I saw a young teen sporting a T-shirt that reads: THE HOOD IS HAPPY. How do you like that?"

*   *   *

"The Golden Rule has entered the housing and building market. Shelter for all is the new goal. Nothing fancy…just decent. Existing properties; commercial and residential, are being converted for residences. There is room for everyone and a home for all. Due to this new excess in unoccupied residential properties, never-before offered purchase options are being offered to even those at the bottom of the economic scale."

"Prisons, asylums, military facilities, battleships and military transports are some of the properties that are being re-purposed for civilian use. Barracks and training camps are being made over into civilian parks and neighborhoods. Until our existing inventory of real estate is used up, the need for new structures and facilities will be greatly reduced. Opportunities in construction are being offered to all willing to work. From learning a trade skill to computer-aided-design to office work, multiple careers are open to all."

"Good work, Annabelle. Keep me informed of further changes on the real estate front."

"You got it, Boss."

"Dave, I want you to work with Cliff Brandon, our chief finance reporter. What could be more important than the plague's effect on money? Is that all right with you Dave? Talk to me. Are you okay with this?"

"Yes Boss. I'm okay with covering the impact of the plague on capitalism, in general. I'll get right on it. And Nat, I'm sorry I doubted you."

"No problem, Dave. You're still my number one reporter. Now get out of here. We both have work to do."

My number one reporter. Nat called me his number one reporter. This is wonderful. I'm so happy, I could cry.

Dave needed to hear that. Having dropped out of college before graduating, he needs regular confirmation that he can do his job. He relies on Nat for continued support.

"Cliff, this is Dave Miller. I just had a conversation with Nat. He wants us to work together on the plague's effect on capitalism. Are you okay with this?"

"I've got to admit, I wasn't comfortable with it when Nat first mentioned it to me."

"Son-of-a-gun. That sly old geezer. He already spoke to you about us working together."

"I'll give you the local take on post-plague finance and you couple that with a global approach, and I think we can do some great reporting. Are we on the same page?"

"Sure, Cliff. Whatever you say. It works for me."

"What happens to capitalism? Could a monetary system based on fear, greed and singular accumulation, and ongoing consumption, transform itself into something new — something possibly called benevolent capitalism? How is post-plague capitalism different from previous capitalism, as we have traditionally known it? Can individuals still amass fortunes?"

"You know Cliff, I don't ordinarily share my byline with anybody, but I think we can work together. How do you feel about it?"

"I feel the same way you do, Dave. I'm not used to sharing my byline with anyone else either. However, since Nat has made it clear that we have no choice and, since I respect you as an investigative journalist, I'm comfortable giving it a try."

* * *

"You guys have had the three days I could wait for a story. What did you find out?"

Nat may be a slave driver, but his quick sense of humor and his continued support outweigh any pushy, hard-work issues.

Everybody likes Cliff, with his close-cropped salt-and-pepper hair, his black-rimmed glasses and his penchant for colorful bowties. His non-threatening demeanor and his 'preppy' appearance ensure his friendship to all. He and Dave look like they could be fraternity brothers; Cliff being the more formal of the two.

"You go first, Cliff."

"Accumulating money, to our surprise, is not being looked at with loathing. Traditionally, aspiring to great wealth or being wealthy was seen as selfish and greedy by the masses. Since the plague, wealth has become a tool to help those less fortunate. With fear and anger having been replaced by unconditional love, being wealthy has actually become attractive; in that using it for the benefit of others has become a joyous civic duty."

"Anything that sticks in your mind, Dave?"

"Warren Buffet's 'The Giving Pledge' is more popular now than ever. It's not just for billionaires any more. People of significantly lower wealth levels are signing up for it."

"Up 'til now, fear-based societies, like ours, spent excessive amounts of money on stress-related maladies. Our individual and collective costs for mental health issues, physical injuries, chemical dependency and abuse have been staggering. The costs of a whole range of crimes against people, property and institutions have been in the trillions."

"Remember now, the plague is worldwide. We're talking of issues on a global scale. The cost of unnecessary incarceration and wasted lives has been off the charts, when calculating losses to the individual and society. Monies and resources allotted to security, defense, prisons, our courts, weapons, law enforcement, counseling, and legal fees can now be re-directed to our infrastructure, our neediest citizens and the betterment of our culture in general."

"Without raising taxes, there is a general fund available that's never been available before. With money for every conceivable need, both individual and collective, on hand, for the first time we may be in a position to eliminate taxes all-together. We are in the unique position to literally build a new world...as we wish. With fear and greed out of the picture, societal changes happen quickly.

There's no manipulating, no backroom deals and no need for committee after committee. Work gets done with lightning speed. There's no red tape to cut through, no pay-offs to make. If an idea is good for the people, it gets done."

"Yes, indeed, Nat. The best price, up-front, is now presented for all goods and services. Used-car salespeople are being looked at with new, more respectful, eyes. With the main force behind wealth transformed into a tool to serve others, fear of the wealthy and powerful by the masses is no longer an issue. Fear of the poor, by the wealthy, is also a non-issue. Evidence is pointing to living to consume being replaced by consuming only what you need to live. Green technology is mushrooming everywhere. It looks as if man-made global warming is fast becoming a non-issue."

"When it comes to employment, job opportunities abound. Mass death has left mass opportunities for the survivors. Of course, numerous job openings have to be tempered with the fact that there are now three billion fewer consumers for all goods and services. Somehow, these two antagonistic situations will even out our work force. Also, factored in here is the widening gap between rich and poor. There is a new attitude in the wind that favors a more equitable distribution of wealth. It does look as though we just might be headed for full employment for the first time ever."

"One final thought, Nat. As an economist, I want to state for the record, I think Thomas Malthus was wrong. The masses that will always be with us need not be poor and disenfranchised. The best investment around always has been and always will be people. And, the return on this investment is immense."

"Cliff, I want to thank you for so graciously allowing Dave to work with you. Dave, your ongoing assignment is to track other changes to our society. So, get with it, and give me the rest of the story ASAP. Thanks again, guys, you did great. Oh, by the way Cliff, I love the new bow tie."

* * *

Even a seasoned reporter like Dave Miller had no idea where this story would lead. No time or place in history could be of help. As long as there have been humans, there has been fear. Where you find fear, you find anger, greed, violence and war. This is "a horse from a different garage", so to speak. Dave remembers his studies of Buddhism and its elimination of the *three poisons* — anger, greed and ignorance.

* * *

What a beautiful woman. I wonder if she's married. And, I can see by the degrees on her wall, she's quite the accomplished shrink. She's got more degrees than my whole office. Bright and beautiful. What a combination.

"Hi, Dr. Terri, my name's Dave Miller, I'm a reporter with the Daily Chronicle. I called yesterday for an appointment. Thanks for seeing me so quickly."

"My pleasure Mr. Miller. What can I do for you?"

"Dave, please, Mr. Miller sounds so formal."

"Okay, Dave, and you can call me Ellen What can I do for you? Please, come sit over here by me."

"I'm writing a story on the changes in society since the plague. I don't mind telling you that there have been some surprises already. What I'd like to know about from you is the plague's effect on the medical profession. I contacted you because you're a recognized leader in the field of mental health."

"Well, Dave, it's really early to see the long-range effects of the plague. That having been said, some obvious changes are so pronounced that I suppose I could shed some light on them —Take drugs, for example."

Dr. Terri giggles.

"I don't mean that you should take drugs."

"I understand completely Dr., Terri…I mean Ellen."

Is she flirting with me? Why is she taking off her jacket? If I wasn't married, I'd be all over her.

"Yes, well, drug use is down, way down. In fact, if it keeps going down at its current rate, by the end of the year we could see a drugless society. I'm not talking about painkillers for legitimate aches and pains. I'm referring to abused and misused escapist drugs like Xanax, Zoloft, OxyContin, Percocet and Prozac. Also, cocaine, opium and heroin use is plummeting. Our long-running war with opioid addiction is quickly disappearing. With fear no longer a dominant force in the world, people feel free to just be. The need to compete, on all levels, is disappearing. However, this drop in competition is being balanced by a rise in higher self-esteem and personal excellence."

"The most prevalent fear, that of failure, is finally gone…and good riddance. People have forever been afraid of not measuring up to some ridiculous, unrealistic, arbitrary, man-made standard. This has influenced peoples' choice of career, spouse, social behavior and more. When you think about it, as I have, this one fear, that of failure, has been responsible for more unhappy, unhealthy, unrewarded lives than any other emotion. That's why I have written about this very subject extensively."

Now that's one fine looking hunk of a man. I see he's wearing a wedding band, but I could get involved with him. With that preppy haircut and collegiate clothes, he must be a Harvard man or maybe Yale. He looks like he teaches on the university level. Maybe journalism? Who knows? He looks good to me. I love the way he twirls his moustache.

"What I hear from my colleagues is that liquor consumption is following the same downward path as drugs. It seems that freedom from fear breeds a healthier and happier population. People feel free to follow their passion; their bliss. There is no longer a need to escape or, to 'take the edge off'. People still strive for a better life, but fear of failure, and its accompanying harshness, seems to be absent. Is this helpful, Dave?"

"Absolutely, Ellen. Please continue."

Damn, she's one good-looking woman. Now she's letting her hair down and shaking it. Even more beautiful. I have got to concentrate. I just can't go through this again.

"Dr. Terri, Ellen, what are you doing? Please don't come any closer."

"Why Dave, are you afraid of me?"

"Please, close your blouse and stay in your chair. I really want to do this interview, but I'll cut it short if you don't stop this behavior."

"Dave, I know I'm being forward, but if you ever decide to 'step out on your wife', you promise to call me. Okay?"

"Fine, Ellen. Now, can we get back to the interview?"

"I'm not used to having men turn me down. Is there something wrong with me?"

"No, there's nothing wrong with you, and you don't need me to tell you that you're beautiful. But, and I mean this seriously, I not only love my wife, I'm in love with her and don't want to do anything that would jeopardize my marriage. Now, back to the interview, please?"

Backing away from Dave and slowly buttoning her blouse, Dr. Terri continues—

"Where was I? Oh, yes, the further you get away from helping others, the closer you get to helping yourself exclusively, and the angrier you become. Allow me to quote Mark Twain: 'Anger is an acid that can do more harm to the vessel in which it is stored than to anything on which it is poured.' The more you focus on helping others, the more inner peace you attain. The truth of this is to be found within. Until now, encouragement to look within has been rare. We have been more likely to seek outside ourselves for answers to life's important questions. Monasteries and monks are in high demand these days. So are seminars in yoga and other forms of meditation. All in so short a time."

"We live in a 3-Dimensional physical world of duality — up/down, in/out, black/white, male/female, hot/cold, rough/smooth, yin/yang and... you get the point. Our feelings lead to our thoughts, which lead to our actions, which come from either love or fear. Being human, we are capable of operating from either position. However, our environment; our culture, has an influence on which position becomes fashionable. When a popular former option, in this case, anger, which is a manifestation of fear, is removed, love prevails. With love as our source, we create an entirely different world from one of fear."

"I can't emphasize this too much, Dave. Did you hear what I just said? Let me repeat it — we create our world. We do not find our world...we create it."

"By the way, Dave, I don't know if you've noticed, but all racial conflicts seem to have disappeared. For the first time in recorded history, we are witnessing the end of racism. The plague brought us all together; in ways we are just beginning to realize. We are all in this together. We are all one. How nice is that?"

"This is important...There is no such thing as a fear gene...or an anger gene. We are not born with a predilection for anger or violence or war. These, we are taught. These are learned. With love in the driver's seat now, how we see the world is changing on a fundamental level. We have empirical evidence, from hundreds of laboratory experiments, that human behavior can be externally influenced to favor a bias to either fear or love. 'We don't see the world as it is; we see the world as we are'. This is especially true when we are innocent and defenseless; as in the formative years."

"You bet, Doc...I mean Ellen. Things are looking up for this old world. If, of course, you can get beyond the speedy demise of one-third of the world's population. I'm not sure where this is leading, but I have a good feeling about it. I thank you for your input. I'll be sure to credit you in my story."

"I wish you well with your article, Dave. I hope we bump into each other sometime. I'm free most weekends."

"Thanks, Ellen. I look forward to meeting you again."

But, not alone. I'm flattered by Dr. Terri's obvious friendly interest in me. But, cheating having cost me my first marriage, I'm not about to get involved with any woman outside my current marriage. I not only love Sharon, I'm deeply in love with her. Sharon's attractive enough, but if she looked more like Dr. Terri, I could get used to that.

*   *   *

"Nat, I have the copy for my next column on *Changes Since the Plague.*"

"Great, Dave. I look forward to all your columns but, I must admit, I'm especially interested in your investigation into post-plague society. What have you got?"

Nat always had it in the back of his head that one day he, his paper, would win a Pulitzer, for investigative reporting. He could feel that day approaching as the words of praise began to filter in about his paper's series on the plague.

"Prisons are quickly becoming obsolete. They're being re-purposed into workshops, offices, artist's studios and group housing, among other things. Concurrent with that, sales of security systems, locks and safes of all fashions are no longer needed. Sales of fences of all kinds have taken a dive."

"Other than traffic control, minor safety issues and helping others, law enforcement is becoming a dying profession. Our Cop-bots are being re-programmed into a kind of Salvation Army/ service organization, for all in need."

"The across-the-board adoption of 'sleeper bullets', not only in the U.S., but globally, shows a greater regard for confrontations between the police and some of our mentally challenged and now-dwindling population of homeless people. This new type of bullet allows the officer in a confrontation to not hesitate to use his weapon, and thereby jeopardize his own safety or the safety of nearby citizenry. When suspicious, he shoots. Period."

"Sleeper bullets don't kill or even injure the targeted person...or animal. On penetration, they disperse a quick-acting drug that puts the suspect to sleep...with no injury. It is proving itself humane and safe. Even a stray shot that hits an innocent bystander, will only render that person temporarily asleep. I wish we'd had this technology years ago. How many wasted lives it could have saved?"

"Most conflicts these days are between man and animal. Remember, at the height of the plague, some wild animals escaped their zoo enclosures. These are quickly being rounded up."

"That's pretty interesting stuff. I wouldn't have imagined that."

"It's just the latest from Shel Kasing of the NRA."

"This whole series on our post-plague society continues to surprise me, too. I mean, prisons to civilian communities...who would have guessed it?"

"Now that fear and anger have all but disappeared, unconditional love is having tremendous effects on all aspects of society. For instance, an obvious change is in the vastly reduced sale of guns, knives and all sorts of weapons. Nothing surprising in that, but at the same time, with conflict and confrontation on the run, our entire legal profession is turning its attention to less dramatic cases such as corporate law, real estate and an increase in patent searches."

"How about politics, Dave? I suspect major changes."

"And you'd be right, Nat. Huge differences."

"Politics has taken a major hit. With the current emphasis on truly representing one's constituents, it's a whole new ballgame. Lobbying, as we've known it, is dead. The playing field for all special interests is level. People can still petition the government for anything, but no one group or individual has more influence than another. *Dark Money* groups have gone the way of big hair and granny glasses. Their need to have a biased influence on the direction the country takes is no longer relevant. Issues must stand on their own merit."

"Government surveillance is gone and legislation is pending to make it disappear from corporate strategy. Nastiness, in any form, is gone from the political scene. And, rudeness...it's completely disappeared. Why, the approval rate for politicians has gone from single digits to a whopping 86%. Did you ever think you'd live to see this?"

"Nat, do you realize that we've had more change since the end of the plague than in our lifetime? Government is no longer the bottleneck it used to be. Government is actually the initiator of new policy on a daily basis. Congress is finally doing the job it was elected to do. I wouldn't be surprised if 'the Golden Rule' became the newest amendment to the Bill of Rights."

"Keep digging, Dave. The more you find out, the better. And, the quicker you report, the better. We do have our competition from other news sources."

*   *   *

"Sharon, have you got time to listen to my next column? It's pretty interesting stuff."

"I'm all ears, Dave. Let's hear it."

"Who would have thought that houses of worship would lose half of their congregants? Even Islam, the most popular religion in the world, has now dwindled in followers and is on the verge of surpassing all other religions in losing adherents and influence. Only those into choir music, religious study, ceremony and group service to others remain."

"With fear and anger on the run, challenging other religions to justify their views or simply attacking them has become passé. It seems with fear of death and joyless lives no longer prevalent, people are not afraid to let their individuality run rampant. People are becoming their own salvation. Dare I say it? — People are recognizing their own divinity. I'm beginning to think that the world is a much better place since the plague."

"You know Nat and his obsession with sports. Well, when it comes to sports, transitions and transformations are tremendous — Playing strictly for the fun of it has tempered rivalries to a bare minimum. Outstanding performances by individuals and teams continue and are applauded by all. It's just that those who don't carry the day no longer see themselves as losers. Doing your personal best, not besting others, is the new rule. And sports fans...their former hostility to rivals has tempered itself to wholesome team support."

"Religion and sports; traditional crowd gatherers, are on different ground now. People still seem to desire to feel a part of something greater than themselves, but the bitterness of the old days is gone. We all need a dream to give life purpose. That being said, now that people everywhere feel a part of humanity, globally, they're free to pursue their own, personal dream. There's a refreshing lightness to public gatherings. We seem to be able to compete and work collectively, minus the tension. I suppose love is not too strong a word for our new atmosphere."

"For those whose appreciation of life was on the wane, this vicious plague only reinforces our need to be grateful for every breath we take. We need to be mindful of just how precious life is. I know with the loss of my son, on top of all the changes in society, I'm viewing life differently from before. I feel more in touch with my surroundings and more thankful for whatever I have; be it health, relationships, ambition. I think I've grown in ways I couldn't have imagined before the plague."

"Up 'til now, as long as you were alive, aging was mandatory. If you do nothing else, you age. Unfortunately, maturity and wisdom are optional. For these to happen, you have to do something; you have to turn inward, you have to reflect, you have to learn, you have to grow...not grow old, but grow whole."

"I'm happy to tell you, Sharon, the Dave you see before you now is not the Dave before the plague. With all the death I've seen lately, especially the death of my son, I know I'm sadder and wiser. As my detachment from material things, fame, fortune and validation has grown, my attachment, the closeness I feel to you and others, has given me a new feeling of belonging, not to locale, but to people. I had no idea at how distant I had become over the years. Perhaps it goes with the territory. I prefer this new feeling. I have an inner peace I've not known before. I don't ever want to be absent this closeness again. I love you, Sharon, more than I can say. You do bring out the best in me. And for that, I thank you."

"That's wonderful, Dave. I, for one, am overjoyed at this surprising turn of events. In my morgue, I've seen far too many people at their worst — way too much premature death — especially violent death. I look forward to a drastic reduction in corpses and autopsies. For whatever reason the plague happened, we who survived it are reaping a most unexpected positive change to society. I welcome it with open arms."

Dave, a man of many words in his profession as an investigative reporter, opts for a less is more attitude and replies: "Ditto."

* * *

"Dave, come in and have a seat. I congratulate you. It seems that your series on our post-plague society is responsible for a 25% increase in our readership. Our owner, Rupert Bradley, is so pleased with your reporting, he's authorized me to give you a 15% raise. How do you like that?"

"That's wonderful news. I'm pleased to accept the raise. As Confucius said 2,500 years ago: *'Find a job you love and you'll never work a day in your life.'* I'm thrilled to be a reporter. And, to get paid to do what I love is the icing on the cake."

"Although I'm still editing my rough draft on the next column, it's turning out well. All modesty aside, and at the chance of offending the Gods, I'm entertaining the possibility of a Pulitzer here. What do you think, Nat?"

Finally, Dave is the professional I always knew he would become. He's a most deserving investigative reporter.

Nat looks up at the ceiling, closes his eyes, and reclines in his high-backed office chair. After a short pause, he looks at Dave and whispers, "You just might be on to something."

Dave holds his breath. Although he wouldn't describe himself as an ambitious man, the thought of such a prestigious award within his grasp gets his attention. A Pulitzer with his name on it would go a long way to eliminating his long-term feelings of inadequacy as a reporter. This possibility is not to be taken lightly.

Excitedly, Dave moves on to his current column and the effects of the plague on education — His interview with Dr. Becky Fuller, the Secretary of Education, has proven to be a real eye-opener.

*   *   *

"Dr. Fuller, what has been the plague's effect on education?"

"Time will tell but in the short period since the plague ended, there are many changes...and all of them seem to be positive. The new emphasis is on universal education. With English having been adopted as the universal language of the planet, it is much easier to share knowledge for all ages. Congress has promptly doubled the Education budget for this year. All efforts are directed to global literacy. Computers for Earth's entire population are the immediate goal. Education for the love of learning opens the doors to all people, everywhere. We want everyone eligible to explore the external world and the world within."

"To aid in this effort, 'mindfulness' instruction has been added to curricular at all educational levels. Whether formal yoga postures or informal practice, such as 'The Six-Step Path', students at all levels, including university, are being introduced to these stress-reducing activities. This is resulting in better grades, quicker learning due to greater focus, and better health all around. As Albert Einstein said: 'The most beautiful thing we can experience is the mysterious. It is the source of all true art and science...' Now, we finally have the will, and, therefore, the time to explore the mysterious."

"Historically, major breakthroughs and inventions, in almost all areas, do not come from team efforts. They come from individuals; often self-educated, who, over a long period of time, and with limited funding, make major discoveries. It's time for 'personalized' education. Preparing each and every citizen on earth to achieve his or her personal best in an area of choice, and to make all capable of contributing to themselves and others, on a variety of levels, is our new goal."

"In addition to being headed to full employment, for the first time in history, people are gravitating to careers that match their innate gifts and talents, not just to earning power. This trend is empowered by the internet, and courses of all manner, being offered by experts in their respective fields. With the global distribution of computers, expert lecturers in all languages, learning about a personal interest is open to all. This personalization of education begins at an early age. Surprisingly, this has led to a reduction in the use of cell phones. The fear and anti-social influences rampant pre-plague, are no longer an influence on people. Any subject matter imaginable is offered to any and all age levels and intellectual capacities. Learning and growing is king."

"As Kalil Ghibran said: *'Your work should be love made visible.'* The former pressure to succeed in terms of wealth and power is now focused more on encouraging the inner you to emerge. People are no longer afraid to be themselves. They no longer fear failure. And, no one feels the need to excel over others. They, we, all of us just want to be our personal best. Harsh judgment is gone, replaced by forgiveness and acceptance. This is true universal education."

"This puts a complete new spin on standardized testing and the stress that used to accompany it. Greed and power are no longer influencing our career choices. People are following their hearts and not their heads for how to spend their time. Bumper stickers and posters have appeared saying: *"Do What You Love and Love What You Do."*

"A return to nature has risen, and with it, the desire for virtual reality has lessened. Unless you're a professional 'gamer', interest in video games is shrinking quickly. Escapism of all types is vanishing as we speak. The need for psychotherapy is dwindling to next to nothing. Along with universal, free education, adequate food, clothing, and medical is being made available to all. What a wonderful state of affairs."

*   *   *

Dave's next interview segues here into AI. Professor Cirk Boardman of the Danish Institute for Nano-technology has little to say except that —

"Artificial Intelligence and Service-bots, traditionally applied where it will make the most profit, is now being applied, almost exclusively, to where a task is too dangerous or too demeaning for a human to do." Gil Bates of Moon Technologies made it clear that new avenues for his company are on the horizon. This, because the public has lost much of its interest in virtual technology since they have a renewed focus on their own real lives."

"Dangerous occupations like stoop labor, mind-numbing, assembly-line work, test pilots, commercial fishing, logging, roofers, garbage men, farmers & ranchers, structural iron & steel workers, truckers, electrical power line installers & repairers, and taxi drivers and chauffeurs are just some of the careers where AI is being focused due to the high incidence of stress and other safety issues."

"Of course, nano-technology will continue to be taken internally to monitor our health on a sub-atomic level. We've had so much success with this proactive regimen that we see no need to discontinue it."

"Driverless cars have already taken over the taxi and limousine business. Those handicapped or temporarily or permanently, in need of assistance, 24/7, can obtain Service-bots, free of charge, through their universal health coverage. With the wide use of driverless cars, the United States alone is saving one million lives a year not killed in auto accidents. Fifty million auto-related injuries have also been avoided."

"Our new emphasis on self-expression and personal satisfaction is taking over from a former focus on income...regardless of safety. We can apply AI any place we choose. And, we now choose to use it to protect and enhance our humanity...not to exploit it. As Mark Zuckerberg promised back in 2016, we are using AI to manage all diseases. Technology will evolve no matter what. What is needed now to accompany this AI evolution is evolved human beings. Better humans, who will be better equipped to interact with, and to build, better machines."

*   *   *

"To paraphrase noted psychologist Abraham Jung: With renewed interest in self-education and creativity, the public has lost interest in many areas of escapism. For example, sales of virtual reality goggles are down. Prescription drugs and alcohol are getting less popular by the day. Gambling is down. Spectator events are down, as the number of performers is growing. People are taking control of their lives and living them to the hilt. These same new changes have been seen in economics, religion and entertainment."

"Let me tell you what I found out about senior citizens. Some of the changes are regional and some are global. Societies where age has always been respected, even revered, have remained much the same. By contrast, youth-oriented societies, like ours, have seen drastic changes."

"For the first time in some 200 years, seniors are being looked to for their wisdom and even as role models. Seniors have even stopped trying to keep up with young people. Trends in fashion, music, language and entertainment for the youth of our nation are staying with them, and not being adopted by their elders. And, although non-seniors still lead trends in race, the environment and green technology, our senior citizens are not far behind."

"With a new value being placed on life experience and wisdom, denying seniors employment because they're "over-qualified" (a term for too old) is going. Age discrimination is dying. Some young people have even begun to dress like our seniors. A newfound respect for their elders seems to be leading to a respect for people of all ages."

"As an added benefit to seniors, free courses in school and online offer daily instruction in how to prepare for retirement and how to navigate said retirement. Our senior population is learning to loosen ties to their earlier career path and to identify with current post-retirement, activities. Seniors are being taught to find meaning and purpose in their later years. They're learning to grow whole, not old. Retirement, as it has been referred to in the last one hundred years, is being completely re-evaluated. It is being seen as the next step in one's life-path, not the final step."

"Nat, this column on society since the plague is on its way to becoming a book, or even a series of books. It's been a real eye-opener to see, day-by-day, how much of our society was fear-based. Most of how we lived, worked and prospered has had to be re-evaluated and re-oriented. Self-discovery leads to self-expression. With love as our collective motivator now, creativity is the prevailing path at all levels. Although challenges remain, conflicts do not. Invention is thriving, with mass creativity encouraged. Everyone knows, for the first time, that they have as much right to apply creativity where they see fit as anybody else."

"I can't help thinking about what Mark Twain said about the purpose of life — *'The two most important days in your life are the day you were born and the day you find out why.'* People are now anxious and pleased to find out why they are here; their personal mission. Self-esteem has taken off like a rocket. Joy is to be found everywhere. People are thrilled just to be themselves. Finding your own important work, finding hobbies and finding your spiritual roots have all become commonplace."

"I'll tell you what, Dave. You keep investigating and writing for the Chronicle, and I'll see about getting you a great deal with a major publishing house. And, who knows, there just may be a Pulitzer in our future."

"Thanks, Nat. I appreciate your complete support for my work. You were right when you said I could take over from Blake. This is the most exciting reporting I've ever done. And, it goes on and on. Every day I discover new changes in society. For the most part, they're all changes for the better. Actually, I can't think of one change that's not for the better. My newest foray is in medicine."

"Stress, the leading cause of illness, is becoming a rare affliction. This is due, in great part, to the introduction of mindfulness training into our education system. From elementary school through college, students and faculty are immersing themselves in this focus-enhancing, stress-reducing practice. This is having a major impact on the medical profession. Dr. Bruce Lipton's work in epigenetics has been thoroughly integrated into our school curriculums and our businesses. What it supports is our personal involvement in what kind of human being we want to be."

"By 2040, Max Moore's Transhumanism Movement of 2017 had morphed into much more than the improvement and enhancement of our physical bodies. Hacking the human body to enhance the body's natural abilities, even when done without medical assistance, proved itself to be of minor importance."

"This is not to downplay its obvious importance in treating cancer, Parkinson's, Hepatitis B, high cholesterol, cystic fibrosis, and other maladies. The movement's efforts to power and control implants, prosthetics and exoskeletons is a no-brainer. Even the use of artificial blood is an accepted advancement."

"However, all this technological gadgetry, especially life extension, becomes irrelevant if one's HQ (happiness quotient) is not improved or enhanced. Life extension is a technological gift. But, without a high HQ, what's the point? More life of suffering is neither attractive nor desirable. All technological breakthroughs aside, the post-plague emphasis on inner peace and the subsequent elimination of anger is what has led us all to our current heaven-on-earth world society."

"With stress on the run, the few remaining needs for the medical profession are orthopedics for the now infrequent injury, optometry, a minimum of relatively minor maladies, and pediatrics and gynecology."

"With the help of computers and nano-technology, all of our diseases are now being managed. The pharmaceutical industry is going the way of fossil fuels. Drug sales are sinking to a historic low. There is no longer a need to escape one's reality. The popularity of booze of all kinds is plummeting. People are content, no, make that happy to be themselves and, aware and alert to the wonders of just being alive."

"People realize that with all these changes, life isn't going to be rosy all the time. They realize that sad events and obstacles to growth and happiness will always exist. Yet, the collective attitude is one of optimism. Overall, people are looking to the future with expectations of success. In spite of struggle and periodic sad tidings, happiness is on the upswing."

"In short, people are no longer afraid to make wrong decisions. They see it as a part of life, not to be feared, but dealt with. They are getting accustomed to being the best they can be...not *the* best, just their personal best. This plague has caused us to re-evaluate success and failure. By individualizing both, especially success, we are becoming better human beings. We are evolving in ways we couldn't have imagined before the plague."

* * *

"Sharon, I've missed you. I get so tied up in my work these days that I forget about everything else. I do miss you, you know. And, I do love you. What do you say to a little break in our work? Let's just go out for dinner...some place nice."

"Why Dave, are you asking me out on a date? After five years of marriage. This is refreshing. Does this mean no talking shop?"

"Not necessarily. I do want to know what's doing at the morgue these days."

"We went from being overrun with anorexic corpses by the hundreds to an occasional autopsy of an obvious natural death.

Other than that, I might just find myself unemployed in the near future. I'm thrilled that I found a cure for the plague, albeit a little late. We don't even know why it stopped, except that with three billion fewer angry people in the world, the tipping point reversed. What do you think? And now to you — how's the writing going?"

"Nat couldn't be happier with my work. In addition to my recent raise, he's promised to look into having my work nominated for a Pulitzer. He says my recent series on The Plague is some of the finest reporting he's ever read. He even called me his number one reporter. He's also promised to see about getting my work seen by a major publishing house. And the work just goes on and on. We've had more changes in how we operate as a society in the past six months then in the preceding 20,000 years."

"The world just isn't working as it has been for the length of history. This is not your father's world, nor his father's before him. To my knowledge, the world has never known a time without fear and its resulting anger, violence, conflict, war and continuous stress of all kinds. We're entering new territory, now. It's going to take time to learn how to live this way."

"And now, enough shop-talk. Put on a nice dress and let's enjoy a special dinner."

"It's been so long since we took time for ourselves, I don't know what to wear."

"Try this on. Perhaps this will give you some guidance."

"Oh, Dave. I don't know what to say."

"Here, let me put it on you."

Dave clasps the shiny, silver chain with its handcrafted pendant around Sharon's neck.

"It looks beautiful. You look beautiful. Get dressed and we'll be on our way."

I didn't know life could be this way. If this is a sign of things to come, then sign me up. This plague seems to be a godsend. It just might be what the world has needed for a long time. Dave and me on a date. How romantic.

"Sharon, did I tell you how beautiful you look?"

"Yes, you did, but please, tell me again."

*   *   *

"A date, a present and dinner out at the city's finest steak house. What's next...a round-the-world cruise?"

"Hold that thought."

"Hello, Dave.

"Hello, Dr. Terri. Nice to see you."

"This is my wife, Sharon. Sharon, this is Dr. Terri, the psychiatrist I told you about."

"He was a perfect gentleman during our interview and completely professional. When I started to come on to him, he made it crystal clear that he is devoted to you and not open to an infidelity of any sort. You're one lucky woman."

Now why did she say that? Does she think I suspect something?

"Do you come here often, Dr. Terri?

"Yes, as a matter of fact, I do. Oh, I see my date, now. Good running into you and, a pleasure meeting you, Sharon. Bye"

"Now I know why you didn't mention how beautiful Dr. Terri was. You had sex with her, didn't you? Don't answer that. And this necklace and fancy dinner out are because you feel guilty. Just like your first marriage. You men. God! You're all alike."

"Sharon, I didn't mention it because, it's irrelevant. You're my love and you're beautiful too. Dr. Terri is simply a source for my investigations into the influences the plague is having on society."

"Are you telling me that you weren't attracted to her during your interview?"

"There's no denying that Dr. Terri is very attractive. But, you know that infidelity cost me my first marriage? I'm not about to let that happen again. Besides, I not only love you Sharon, I'm in love with you. That should count for something."

"Sharon, please, this is supposed to be a date, for just the two of us. I don't want anything to interfere with it. Since the arrival of the plague, I've had to overcome my claustrophobia, my acrophobia, my fear of being lead reporter for the Chronicle and the test of my faithfulness to you, by interviewing Dr. Terri. Of all of these tests, I'm most proud of my resistance to Dr. Terri. Believe me, Sharon, I am truly in love with you...and only you. Let's just order and get on with the evening...with our evening."

"You're right, Dave. Please forgive me. She just shouldn't be so damn beautiful."

"A toast...to us and our future together."

"I'll drink to that. And, by the way, I want to thank you for the contribution you made in my name to my alma mater. It was very sweet of you and means a lot to me."

* * *

"Hi, Jay. Nice of you to see me on such short notice."

"Come in. It has been a long time. I do think of you when I reflect on my, make that our, high school days. And, I've been reading your column in the Chronicle. Very nice work. You should think about writing a book on this plague situation."

"Funny you should mention that. My editor said the same thing just yesterday. Perhaps it's time. I'll send you a copy if I do it."

"So, Jay, the plague has affected many areas of our society— medicine, education, real estate, career moves, money and commerce, and more. What I'd like from you is a rundown on its effect on our judicial system...if any."

"We're in the process of overhauling our entire judicial system, as we speak. With fear and anger gone, winning is no longer of prime concern. Lawyers and courts have turned their attention from an adversarial one to truth finding. Lawyers for the prosecution now share all evidence with lawyers for the defense. When the truth of the case is revealed, both sides rejoice. The prison system is on its way to becoming a relic of the past. With fear gone, the crime rate is virtually non-existent. Early-release programs are going national. No, make that global."

"Creativity is running rampant. People, who never considered that they had anything to offer the world, are inventing new devices, machines, tools for all sorts of operations and copyrighting new ideas, formulas and stories. This is where my colleagues and I come in. The demand for patent searches is going through the roof. The control that fear had on individuals and groups to perform well or to create anything is no longer a factor. People are not afraid to try something new; be it a food, a method or an idea."

"It makes me think of Thomas Edison, who, when asked by a nervy, young reporter, if he didn't feel stupid for failing 10,000 times to make an incandescent bulb. Without hesitation, Edison replied: 'Of course not...I learned 10,000 ways not to do it.' Fear of failure is dead. May it never return."

"I'm telling you, Dave. It's a whole new world out there. The sky's the limit on people's ability to think, act, create and assemble the world they desire. We lawyers are still needed to work out contracts, cover creations, negotiate deals, and, of course, handle real estate. But, the focus is no longer on how many hours a month are being billed."

"An increased portion of our business is estate planning and the settlement of existing estates. We've had to double our staff in this area. With all the victims of the plague, millions of households have estates that need to be settled now. Most of our victims were part of an estate. Also, divorce...not contested, nasty divorce, but amicable, mutually agreed upon separation. The days of the court as a battlefield are over. As a place of inquiry and discovery, yes, it is still necessary. But, as a place for justice denied and the abuse of power...that appears to be a thing of the past."

"Thanks, Jay. This is exciting news, and good news. It's a true reflection of the transformation of our society from a basis of fear to one of love. It's truly amazing...and long overdue. Thanks for your input."

"You're welcome, Dave. Good to see you. Let's not get out of touch again."

"You're right, Jay. I'll call you soon. Thanks for your help."

*   *   *

"Steve Georgeson of Channel 10 News here, with my special guest Senator Sandy Bernstein. Senator Bernstein, welcome to our show."

"Thank you, Steve, a pleasure to be here."

"Senator, I understand you have proposed a reform bill in the Senate...a bill influenced by what you call, "The Angry Plague."

"Yes, George, that's correct. My bill, dubbed *The Grassroots Manifesto*, will bring sweeping changes to our country and, if successful here, the world."

"Senator, I've read your bill and it raises some serious questions. If you would be so kind to highlight your bill here, I'll present these questions, one at a time. Is that okay with you?"

"Certainly, Steve. My bill is as follows." —

"How a society treats its least capable and most dependent members is an accurate measure of its level of fear and anger. How it cares for its least fortunate and most needy citizens reveals its worthiness to be called great."

"Opportunities offered on a universal level are clearer indicators of a society's humanitarian structure. For example, is it meeting the five basic needs of all of its citizens? Does it provide adequate food, clothing, shelter, medical attention, and education to all? Not superior, not luxurious, but simply adequate."

"When these five programs are firmly established as guaranteed rights (not privileges), whether one parlays them to great heights or not, is irrelevant. Their availability to all, alone marks a culture as truly advanced and free of fear."

"As you wrote in one of your columns, 'Historically, major breakthroughs and inventions do not come from team efforts. They come from individuals, who, over time and with limited funding, make major discoveries and inventions. Therefore, preparing each and every individual to achieve his or her best in personal areas of choice makes all capable of contributing to themselves and others on a variety of levels.'"

"I'm flattered that you've taken the time to read my column."

"Don't sell yourself short, Dave. Your columns on our world, post-plague, have been informative and well-written. Now, where was I?"

"If, to this guarantee of five basic rights is added a judicial system that is not adversarial, but one united in its search for truth, the society created will be both capable and just. This is a society that can support and care for itself. This is a sign of a culture not based on fear."

"The kind of society proposed here costs no more and most likely, less, than our past cultural arrangement, which is exorbitantly costly. A fear-based arrangement has excessive expenses for stress-related maladies, mental health issues, physical injuries, chemical dependency and abuse, and a whole range of crimes against people, property, and institutions and, in the final analysis, wasted lives."

"And how do you propose that we pay for this change in services?"

"Unaffordable amounts of money have traditionally been spent on security, defense and prisons. It costs between $75,000 and $250,000 per year, to incarcerate one prisoner — food, clothing, housing, courts, weapons, counseling, legal fees, etc."

"And, most of those incarcerated pursued a criminal path because of a lack of opportunity and hope. A large prison population is the predictable response to despair, anger and violence."

"Senator, what about lost jobs? Your proposal, even if affordable, will cost millions of people in law enforcement, prison services and a whole host of related legal careers, their jobs. What happens to these people currently employed?"

"I'm glad you asked that, Steve. With universal education and re-training, career opportunities offered in my bill will leave no one unemployed...or, for that matter, unemployable. Whether it's mining or recreation, in either arctic region of our planet or on the moon or Mars, every opportunity possible is open to all."

"Let me make this clear, what we teach our children and what behaviors we encourage in people at all levels, gets reflected in the kind of society we have. The world is not so much as we find it, but as we make it."

"Funny you should state it that way. You're not the first person I've interviewed who said that." — 'The world is what we make it, not how we find it'.

"That is so true, Dave. The system I am advocating, in addition to offering a joyful atmosphere of vastly reduced stress, opens the door to a society of healthy, creative and constructive individuals. It is easier and cheaper to proactively thwart problems than to have to foot the bill to clean up and solve problems after the fact.

It's not a question of whether to spend money and resources or not. It's a choice of spending less now with fewer problems later (the moral high ground) or to spend more, later, on resulting problems that needn't have arisen at all."

"As Cliff Brandon, your paper's economics reporter, wrote:" 'Malthus was wrong, — the masses that will always be with us need not be poor, needy and disenfranchised. The best investment around always has been and always will be people. And, the return on this investment is immense."

"As a result of the plague, let's get on to the next level of evolution, to a social consciousness that values and invests in its citizens — for the immediate and long-range benefit of all."

"Thank you, Senator Bernstein. If your *Grassroots Manifesto* is adopted, and, since the plague ended, it seems to be sure to pass in both houses of Congress, we're going to get to see what effect this 'New World Order' has on our society."

"Well, there you have it folks. It looks as if we the people have a second chance at creating the world in which we live. Thanks, and good night. This is Steve Georgeson of Channel 10 News signing off."

                        *   *   *

"Nat, here is my latest column — Our infrastructure is being refurbished and updated, daily — not for profit, but because it needs to be fixed. This makes available enough job opportunities to get us, for the first time, to zero unemployment. The insurance industry is in the grip of major changes. Actuarial tables are now being used to maximize benefits to clients, not to maximize profits. War is no longer a career-choice. It's not good for business any more. The Salvation Army, now non-sectarian, has become the new 'army' of choice."

"We are sending our expanded Salvation Army troops to all corners of the globe; to help in our collective war on poverty, lack of education and access to clean water and medicine. As you can see in this holo-vid, we are welcomed everywhere. Parades and celebrations are held in our honor on a daily basis. Our work with all nations and factions has changed the world's mindset, from intrusion to support, from invasion to all kinds of aid, and from enemy to long-term friend. Our ranks are swelling geometrically."

"With a budget of just under $600 billion, one of the areas hardest hit by this queer turn of events, and now embarking on a huge overhaul, is the military. With fear relegated to the dustbin of history, cleaning house is currently large-scale. Destroying or retrofitting military installations is a popular solution to updating old properties."

"The Book of Isaiah 2:3-4 has been heard throughout the halls of Congress and on the streets – *'...and they shall beat their swords into plowshares and their spears into pruning hooks...and they shall learn war no more.'* We're not talking just the Pentagon. This new theme is global in scale. Can you imagine? No more anger means no more war. I wouldn't mind reporting good news for a while."

"Except for a slightly enlarged Coast Guard and a slight increase in the use of Soldier-bots, a career in the military has all but vanished. The Joint Chiefs are being disbanded and the military-industrial complex that Eisenhower warned of is going. The Pentagon is being retrofitted to be the largest university in the world. The vast military budget is now a surplus that can be dispersed back to the citizens in many ways or used to aid nations in need. Part of it is funding our recent increase in recruits for the Salvation Army."

"I tell you, Nat, every day the old is being transformed into the new. I'm beginning to wonder if there is an end to changes in our society. People are expected to live longer now, because they want to. Suffering from 'Kiroshi', the Japanese label for a person who works himself to death, is over"

"Factories that can't be retrofitted, are being gutted and the real estate sold. Military equipment that can't be used for non-military purposes is being sold or destroyed. Camp David is being re-purposed into a rehab facility for the handicapped. Nuclear missiles and their delivery systems are being dismantled."

"When it comes to entertainment, attendance at bars is vanishing. In addition to not needing to soften life, people are too busy exercising their newfound right to be creative. New, enjoyable careers, new hobbies, a newfound passion for being alive are all flourishing. Local venues of all kinds are sprouting up everywhere; artists, craftspeople, writers, singers, photographers, dancers, musicians, actors, and performers of all categories are blossoming. The same for inventors and tinkerers at all levels."

"Travel, local and global, has increased tremendously. With former restrictions of all kinds removed and safety a non-issue, people are visiting people everywhere. Best travel deals are to be found on the internet and in local papers. Truth in advertising is now slanted to facts, before sales. With profits to a minimum, travel is now more affordable for all."

"Money and wealth of all kinds is being re-examined and re-evaluated. Our 'old' economy, based on an ever-increasing amount of consumption of goods and services, is being replaced by a 'new' economy, based on caring and sharing. The gap between rich and poor is quickly closing. We will no longer use our material wealth as our sole measurement of success, satisfaction and enjoyment. We are going way beyond the phrase, 'He who dies with the most toys wins.'"

"Before the plague, the middle-class had pressure 24/7. Either they were in danger of falling behind economically and faced the scary possibility of dropping into the world of the lower-class ghetto dweller, or, they had to deal with the relentless pursuit of upward mobility into the upper-middle class or even the upper class. This push-pull lifestyle of constant stress had its deleterious effect on people of all ages caught in this in-between status."

"This of course was before the plague. Since the plague, the stress level of the middle-class is almost nil. Why? Because falling to the lower class is no longer judged a failure. With the ghettos now safe and under an attractive transformation of the physical plant, life there is rather pleasant. While all are encouraged to do their best and to be their best, without competing with others, one's address is no longer a consequence for advancement or condemnation."

"With the enacting of Senator Bernstein's Five-Step program, those with lesser incomes have support for their efforts, as needed. No one is faced with societal abandonment. If the desire for advancement is present, appropriate encouragement and support is also present in equal measure. I'm telling you, Nat, ours is a new, and better world; certainly, a more equitable world than one could have hoped for. For the first time in history, the future looks bright for all of Earth's people."

"Of necessity, the media — print and video, has all but given up tabloid journalism and replaced that sort of reporting with good news. The time-honored catchphrase of the media: 'If it bleeds, it leads.' has been replaced by 'If it serves needs, it leads.' Hyperbole, self-serving rhetoric and bias are being replaced by true and validated reporting. Ambush journalism is passé. Celebrating talent and good works is in. Embarrassing moments and fashion faux pas are out."

"Nat, all of the good news notwithstanding, I feel the need to end this series with a note of caution."

"What are you talking about, Dave? After reporting a seemingly endless series of good news, how could you have doubts about our future?"

"With fear, anger and greed on their deathbed, the new paradigm of love and compassion promises a brighter future for humankind than ever previously imagined. That being said, I have a gnawing feeling that something is amiss. I know, life is infinitely better now. I've witnessed it. I've reported it. With an end to fear, anger, war and, surprisingly, most illnesses, life here on Earth is a virtual paradise. We finally understand that our most precious resource is people."

"I don't mean to sound like a party-pooper, but to paraphrase, 'uneasy lies the life without conflict.' Can we really understand love without fear in the equation? How do you learn about courage without fear to transcend? With no 'bad guys' anymore, excuses for poor behavior are non-existent. With no obvious, negative enemy to conquer or transcend, Pogo may have been right, 'We have seen the enemy, and he is us.' The only foe we have to overcome now is ourselves. I suspect that this has always been the case. It's just that now, there's no avoiding it."

"No fear. No anger. There's nothing in the way of behaving good and living the life we're meant to. We just have to follow our hearts and do our best. Not to sound ungrateful, I just feel that something is missing. I see the changes; changes for the better, all around me. Good changes. The world is better off without fear and anger."

"As an aftermath of the plague, if we don't learn to be grateful for every minute we have on this earth from now on, we never will. I know I have. I think I'm finally beginning to understand the Eastern philosophy I've been studying all these years. Having survived the plague, I'm grateful for every minute of life. We've been given a second chance, here. I hope everyone left alive learns to appreciate the brief time they have and to make the most of it. If we learn nothing else from this pandemic we had better learn that we must evolve as a species; we must become better people."

"I'll keep digging. Maybe something will turn up. I hope it doesn't. Dave Miller signing off."

*   *   *

(2133 AD)

"Reggie Miller of Channel 3 News here folks. Welcome to New Year's Eve, 2133 and our annual Post-Plague Parade of Happiness. As you can see, millions of people line Fifth Avenue here in New York. The young, the short and the handicapped are in front, as well they should be. Order, quiet and peace reign, as usual."

"Mom, you and Grandma sit up front here, in your hover-chairs. Rachel, you and your brother, sit next to Grandma, in your anti-grav boots. Jack, you and I and Ralph are the tallest, so we'll stand behind them; supported by our 'stand-ups'. Now, everybody, start your 'holo-corders'."

"As is our custom, The Salvation Army leads our parade. See how proudly they march. They are leaders in selflessly helping others. What a glorious sight. If not for thousands of parades elsewhere, it would take days for the ranks of this army to pass by.

We stand at attention. We salute our Earth-flag, as do others all over the world. We are here, and in all the towns and cities of this great world, to celebrate our freedom from fear. Can you believe it folks? This is our 93rd year of this celebration."

"One can recall the Pax Romana of 2,000 years ago. Even though that lasted for some 200 years, that peace was not a real peace. It was more of a heavy-handed suppression of all dissent. That lack of war was due to an all-encompassing fear, not love. Never in history has there been such a time as ours. Just think about it — No fear, no anger, no violence and no more war; all by choice, not rule. Reporting on all the good news from all over."

"Professor Shuster, the floor is yours." —

"Thank you, Reggie. As all of you know from history class, by 2030, the population of earth had swelled to eight billion people. Although we had the technology to feed all of us, we hadn't the will. Our calculated inequity of distribution wouldn't allow for that. Consequently, food riots erupted on a regular basis. These, coupled with global warming's drastic reduction in clean water and clean air, only speeded up the magnitude and frequency of the riots."

"Mass migrations followed — the result of war, extreme climate changes and the wasting of natural resources. Our insatiable craving for energy from fossil fuels ensured the destruction of our natural environment. By 2040, with a population of nine billion people, our arsenal of self-inflicted wounds had ninety-nine percent of us in dire straits. We were on a collective, suicidal race to extinction. We had reached a global tipping point that triggered a word-wide catastrophe."

"Looking back, as every school-child knows, since 2,040, the Fourth Industrial Revolution, boosted by the Plague, has been a major success in its influence on our world...with Moore's Law rushing it along at an ever-increasing pace. Welcome to The Exponential Age. Education on a global scale has leveled the playing field between all economic classes. Following the Plague, it's been clear that we're all in this together. And, let's not forget the resounding success of Senator Sandy Bernstein's *Grassroots Manifesto.*"

"Good evening. I am Prof. Max Shuster, here to present our 93rd re-cap of life since the Plague. Ever since it ended and we learned the true cause, it's been named The Angry Plague. I call it '*History 101 – The World Post-Plague... A Holographic View.*'"

"Please see your tablet, or read our written series in The Libertarian Times. In this lecture, we will cover the changes and advances in our culture since the Plague. My focus is on the following topics — The Plague's effect on: Stress, Education, Parenting, Government, Transportation, Energy and Artificial Intelligence. Please follow along with me."

"As you know, with the end of anger, we evolved into a stress-free society. This radical change in our environment put an end to physical altercations, vastly fewer accidents and almost no illness. In fact, with stress to a minimum, when feeling out of sorts, self-healing has become the rule. Consequently, the need for doctors has dropped drastically. Various kinds of meditation have replaced all kinds of medication. Hence, the popularity of T-shirts and bumper stickers that read — MEDITATION, NOT MEDICATION."

"Concurrent with this downtrend, except for keeping physically flexible, formal, ritualized regimens of meditation have disappeared. "Big Pharma" has all but gone out of business. Some mind and body enhancing drugs remain, but the pervasive, regular use of prescription "meds" died 93 years ago."

"Since the plague, education has been most revealing. With good physical, mental, emotional and spiritual health the norm, the people of Earth are at peace with themselves and their environment. Having spent a lifetime with mindfulness training of one sort or another, coupled with a reduced workweek, a decent wage, and a handsome package of benefits, people of all ages have little difficulty adjusting to their situation at different stages of life. We've learned to embrace our inner selves and our outer world. Our harmony with life, all life, is deep and sincere. We no longer grow old; we grow whole."

"Health-wise, robot diagnosticians, affectionately known as 'Dr. Kiosk', are everywhere, cost-effective, and 100% reliable. World-class medicine is finally here for all of Earth's citizens."

"This has led to an unbiased atmosphere in our classrooms. All questions are given fair attention and consideration. No agenda, hidden or otherwise, is allowed to skew class content. We firmly believe in John 8:32 – 'The truth shall set you free.'"

"As you know, universal, free education is available to all. Many of the lectures and books, by MIT's Noam Chomsky continue to be studied for ideas on how to run a caring society and avoid the pitfalls of an oppressive one. There is no place internet-free. Presentations, like this one, are open to whoever wishes to join. Grades are unnecessary, as are tests. You choose your own path and you decide to do with your skills as you see best. Notice the T-shirts that say: AN INFORMED PUBLIC IS A CAPABLE PUBLIC."

"This brings us to a most interesting topic; parenting. Traditionally, parenting involved training and coercing our children to be obedient, to follow rules, to learn to be part of the collective. They were encouraged to work hard, especially in school, to get good grades and to compete...on all levels."

"This regimen was used in virtually all cultures, at all times, to ensure the upward mobility of families and their descendants. Marriages were arranged, to secure family wealth and power. Class structure was adhered to in most cultures. This was the way of the world as long as anyone could remember. It was based on fear...of failure, of loss, of being left behind. It was based on the (false) belief that there was not enough to go around, so competing was justified. Violence and war were also justified in such a climate. The result of this climate of fear was universal stress, ill-health, anger and unhappiness."

"The world, post-plague, is unique. Fear is gone. Anger is gone. War has become ancient history. With this de-emphasis on competition; other than with one's self, cooperation has replaced it. Racism, religion and other channels of division, have themselves become obsolete. Self-expression has taken over our value structure...not material wealth and its partner, power. As John Kenneth Galbraith wrote: 'Personal liberty, basic well-being, racial and ethnic equality and the opportunity for a rewarding life are what make for 'The Good Society.'"

"This has left parents with a much simpler mission — Teach your children the Golden Rule and love them unconditionally. Encourage them to discover, release and let blossom their unique gifts and talents, especially in service to others. And, while you're at it, parents, apply these same teachings to yourselves."

"All of us, while not equal in specific abilities and talents, are equal in value. We all have flaws and weaknesses, but we balance these with gifts and talents tailored to each of us. We know we are all born to accomplish something. We now know that purpose and meaning of life is subjective and comes not from any external source, but from within."

"How are we doing, so far? Reggie? Any questions?"

"No, Dr. Shuster, no questions. You seem to be covering our collective past history rather well. So, Dr., please continue."

"Reggie, people of Earth, please follow me as we refresh our glorious history lesson." —

"An example of this global education has led to inventions like that of Danesh Steiner — his affordable, portable, desalinizer and water purifier has resulted in clean, safe water for the entire planet. Whether for drinking or farming, any place with people is a place with good water. Our desalinization plants provide oceans of clean, potable water."

Our improvements in non-fossil fuels, in solar, wind, and geo-thermal provide clean, safe energy for the entire planet. And, with the not-for-profit status of all our utilities, the world is never without free power."

"Harvey Chang's breakthrough with fusion cells has given power to all of us...cheap, safe power. When it comes to medicine, Bernice Mrumba's hand-held health analyzer is used worldwide. "

"We all have a purpose. We only have to find our 'special' purpose and urge it to blossom. If your gifts require 3-dimensional creation of a sculpture or a prototype to be manufactured, the rise of, and access to, 3-D printing is available to all. This opens the door to revised government agencies. Let me introduce Dr. Rachel Nader, the new head of the EPA."

*   *   *

"Thank you, Dr. Shuster. Since the plague, our organization, has concentrated on the global expansion of the Environmental Protection Agency. Our goal of restoring the rainforests to their pre-20th century levels has been a complete success. Equally successful is the return of our arctic-ice and the end of global warming.

Our work with clean water has saved and protected large bodies and small streams of water, both domestic and foreign, from harmful intrusions. Consequently, our formerly dwindling fish populations are back to healthy proportions. Life forms that go extinct now, go by natural selection, not by human intrusion into their environment. Beaches and bodies of water are no longer closed; unfit for human use."

"We are happy to inform you that our eco system is now, and has been for the past 25 years, pollution-free. Our (global) environment is as pure and clean as if we left no footprint at all. This is the first time since the dawning of the Industrial Revolution that we can say this. You will notice, as you look around, you never see someone wearing a surgical mask. Our earth, air and water are pristine and safe."

"All structures, both residential and commercial, have been brought into compliance with the most stringent, global-wide, building standards ever imposed. We strive to protect our citizens and the environment from all pollutants, chemicals and waste intrusion. A safe environment for all creatures on this planet has been achieved."

"Our mandate for a clean environment extends beyond structures. With our newly imposed, strict regulations on the auto industry, our cars, trucks and hovercraft are fully electric, driverless (where desired) and environmentally friendly. They can only improve from here on in. We are working closely with the new Global Recycling Agency for a cleaner, healthier and safer planet. Even our 'space junk' is regularly recycled. Remember, no one is safe until we're all safe."

*   *   *

"The government is pleased to announce the formation of our newest agency. What was formerly the CDC has been transformed into the Office of Health and Happiness. The mission of the OHH is to insure the greatest happiness and inner peace for all; at all ages. It will oversee education, health and interpersonal relations to reduce stress and increase inner peace. With anger out and unconditional love in, we can do this; at home and abroad. We do not mandate; we educate. As the saying goes: 'an informed public is a capable public. We are here to serve.'"

"Through our revised education policies, and our emphasis on self-expression and self-discovery, we see happiness naturally arising from self-fulfillment. We have raised two generations according to these values and the results are indisputable. Exploring and instigating the blossoming of your natural gifts and talents, virtually assures happiness and contentment. Not one instance of bullying has been reported in 93 years. Following your heart and not your head is key here. Believe in yourself and your feelings. We are all one...and one is us."

"Much of our efforts are devoted to global sharing. Those who have much are encouraged to share with those who have little. Living this way justifies our calling ourselves advanced. It also raises our happiness quotient. Our motto: TO SERVE IS TO SATISFY is our pledge to all of Earth's citizens."

* * *

"This government-sponsored, laissez-faire attitude towards education applies as well to economics. With the end of democracy came the rise of what was popular in Scandinavia, Switzerland and the Netherlands in the 20th and 21st centuries. It is called: 'Democratic Socialism'". With the end of the two-party system and the reduction of the 40-hour workweek to 20 hours, we earned the right to call ourselves *advanced.* As every child learns early on — "The freedom to swing your arms ends where another's nose begins." Zechariah Chafee (1919). Live and let live is our motto."

"Now, and for 93 years, we have the most freedom and the least amount of government intrusion. Our need for Social Security began to lessen two generations ago. People, once freed to pursue satisfying, creative work, refused to retire. The opportunity to release their innate talents led to new, unexpected, second and third careers. Older people grew then, and continue to grow, whole, not old."

"To the surprise of many, the rise of altruism under this form of government has been swift and complete. We seem to have earned our status as 'heaven on earth'. With freedom to think, to feel, to be, love truly has triumphed over fear. The mass appeal of self-fulfillment as a 'life's purpose' has cemented this heaven on earth life-style as our proudest achievement."

"Dr. Fuller, let me intrude here for a second. Is there a scientific justification for this massive change in our society?'

"Absolutely, Reggie. But, science with a twist. Here, let me explain." —

"The battle between "Idealism and Materialism" ended with Idealism in the winner's circle. Consciousness is thoroughly accepted now as "a priori", a fundamental initiator of reality. Dr. Robert Lanza was right: "Consciousness creates matter, not the other way around. We now blend with our world "out there" in a loving, creative way that has never existed. We are not compelled to 'fit in'. We are truly blessed. We are not passive, victims of some objective world. We do our part. We take responsibility for our actions. We now know that 'the world is not so much as we find it, but as we make it.'"

"Our 'people first' priority has led to technology second. Since the emergence and overwhelming popularity of driverless cars, (we no longer need a driver's license) more than one million lives per year are being saved. The ubiquitous 'hover-shoe' has become the preferred mode of transportation in highly populated areas. Hovercrafts of different capacities have given us access to all of Mother Nature's most beautiful scenery. (Remember, these crafts leave no footprint.) Speaking of which, by the year 2060, the energy to power these shoes, cars, computers and all other devices became non-fossil, renewable, non-polluting and just plain cheap."

"While we're on the subject; manufacturing, virtually all manufacturing is done with 3D printers. Much of this printing is done in residences with table-top printers."

"This brings us to the last of our topics: Artificial Intelligence. Although predicted by Ray Kurzweil in early 21st century, 'The Singularity' did not take place (expected around 2045). The rendering of humans obsolete did not, and will not, happen."

"Thanks to computer programmer Sam Altman, self-policing software was designed and implemented in all computer-run machines. He and physicist Michio Kaku and their team put a "shut-off" chip in all robot brains."

"As to the humanization of AI, without emotions and feelings, machines have not and will not replace humans, as stated by Prof. David Gelernter of Yale. Regardless of how intelligent our computers/machines/robots become, we, and they, cannot program our non-physical parts; our spirituality, or to put it another way: love. If love is to remain and to prevail, humans are needed to feel it. And, without love, why be alive at all?"

"Physicist Stephen Hawking supported Prof. Gelernter's work. With these monitors in place, dire predictions of a dystopic society, like those predicted by Dr. Nick Bostrom, never materialized."

"As feared by many in the scientific community, geeky technocrats did not triumph. Thanks to the work of a few early scientists and AI creators, a sort of technocratic (think Hippocratic) Oath did prevail. These, at first a few, and later many, programmers, who had not lost their humanity in their scholarship, grew into a majority. We learned you must change people along with technology or, as your technology advances, your undesirable consequences advance proportionately. Soul-less machines were not allowed to take over from humans. There was no rise of the 'terminators'. Robotics serves at the pleasure of all people. People first, AI second. They perform what we want, when we want it and where we want it. They serve us."

"Also, in addition to an 'off' switch on all "C.O.M's" (computer operated machines), the programing of an expiration date (think death), has rendered all machines non-threatening. They may be faster than we humans are and their memories are able to hold and retrieve more data. Yet, they continue to serve us and not the other way around. We are a necessary part of the universe; the cosmic plan. Robots are not."

*   *   *

"Reggie Miller back at the studio. Thank you, Dr. Shuster and Dr. Fuller. Isn't that a summation to be proud of? As usual, all is right with the world. War is still a thing of the past. Territorial wars, ethnic wars and especially religious wars are relics from days gone by. The order of the day, now and for many years, has been goodness. Anger is out and love is still in."

*   *   *

"Back to our parade. Peace symbols are everywhere, as is the word love...on flags, on T-shirts, on banners and even on peoples' faces. Louie Armstrong imitators are marching together and singing "What A Wonderful World". Michael Jackson imitators singing "We Are the World" follow them. A third group of marchers is singing Minnie Riperton's hit, "Lovin' you". The crowd, of course, is singing along with all of them.

Just coming into view is the last active of our seven branches of the military, the Coast Guard. They have proudly served others since their inception and continue to serve all in need."

"Earth's entire population is striving to be good. Our leaders and role models are now the gurus of the past; the spiritualists like Jesus, The Buddha, Moses, Gandhi, Martin Luther King Jr., Mother Theresa, Pope Francis and the Dalai Lama. We respect and learn from those who are familiar with and comfortable with unconditional love. If we are to follow anyone, it's the gentlest, most compassionate and least judgmental among us. We look to be mentored by the most loving of our species. We have traded power over others for mastery of the self. We no longer follow our warriors and power brokers. Love is our weapon of choice."

"For the first time in the history of mankind, everybody is trying to be good. Children are taught from infancy to practice the Golden Rule. Don't forget, the gradual downward spiral of the workweek to our current 20 hours has helped cement our collective happiness. And, much of that work can be done at home or while commuting in a driverless car. Add to this, a lengthy and productive, active, self-fulfilling retirement, and you have a rebirth of the Garden of Eden."

"This is paradise on earth, folks. Food production is ample for the masses, since protein is now grown in giant petri dishes and vegetables are grown hydroponically in weatherproof rooms. This has freed up much land and created an almost non-existent need for cattle. This drastic reduction in cattle has meant a most welcome reduction in gas emissions. These emissions had long been proven a contributor to global warming. Our forests have come back...as have our rain forests and our polar ice. This is success on a global scale. Everyone is jubilant."

"Professor Shuster and Dr. Fuller, please allow me to pose a question. I have been pondering this thought for a long time. With no conflict, isn't there a danger of boredom taking over?"

"I hear you, Reggie. This was the fear immediately following the end of the Plague. With struggle out of the picture, what incentive is there to evolve? Yet, as you see, for 93 years, we have managed quite well. Boredom has not replaced fear."

"May I continue, Reggie?"

"Please, Professor, continue."

"After tens of thousands of years of conflict, people everywhere are being good. Neighbors are helping neighbors. Strangers are going out of their way to help strangers. We are justifiably proud of our achievement of a good society. Surely God is smiling. We are one, global family...on a collective return to the Garden of Eden. Bit-coin is our universal currency. Politics has transformed itself into a respectable and honorable profession, now that all politicians are retina-scanned as they talk — lying is so out."

"Permit me an update on travel — Our wide use of fusion power for our homes, business and travel, coupled with solar and wind power, has kept us alive with cheap power and nonexistent pollution. Our driverless cars, trucks and buses whisk us silently to our destinations. The same for our fusion-powered trains, planes and space shuttles. Travel between Earth, the Moon, and Mars is safe, affordable and pollution-free."

"On the local level, our hover boards and hover boots afford us effortless short-range mobility. We explore to our hearts content and leave a zero-level footprint. Much of this travel takes us out of our high-tech cities. Speaking of cities." —

"Allow me to expand here. Paolo Soleri's environmentally sound cities, Arcosanti being the first of his 'Arcologys', is currently housing groups of 5,000 to 25,000 citizens in each one, all over the world. His work in the desert, north of Phoenix, AZ, from the 1970's on, is now a popular option for urban living."

"These energy-efficient, non-polluting, small-scale cities, allow the inhabitants to live a healthy urban life while exploring a surrounding, untouched, glorious countryside. Our enjoyment of the natural world is unlimited, now that our forests are back to their 18th-century growth. Our buffalo roam free, and our ponds, lakes, streams and oceans are chock full of fish and shell fish."

"This makes zoos obsolete, since our access to wildlife in its natural habitat is within easy reach. We can live wherever we wish: city, suburbia, rural countryside and wilderness. We are connected to all life everywhere. We are truly one people and one life. So, why worry about anything? Remember that popular, 20th-century saying: 'If it ain't broke, don't fix it.'"

"Yes, Professor, I am familiar with that phrase. I know that this is the way it's been for 93 years. And, with stress to a minimum, 125 years is about right for the current life span. Yet, as my grandfather cautioned in his series on the early post-plague Earth, '...something doesn't feel right.' Re-reading my grandfather's columns and books, I wonder just what it was that he was suspicious of. Could it be that without the agony, there can be no ecstasy? Without the struggle, can there be an overcoming? Don't we need a conflict to overcome or a battle to win? As he said: "Can we really understand and appreciate courage without fear?" He wrote something about us living in a world of duality."

"I believe what he meant is that the goal is not to eliminate the negative or difficult side of duality, but to learn to transcend that part of the equation. With nothing to rise above, our purpose here on earth may be irrelevant."

"I think there's more here to be understood. I have some research to do. I'll let you know what I find. "Since the Industrial Revolution, our technological advancement has been significant and ever-increasing. With all this impressive achievement, are we any happier? Are we basking in inner peace? We are decidedly not. So, of what value is all this progress? It leaves a bad taste in its wake. Perhaps, before, and during, all this advancement, people had the right to look to technology as a panacea. They could not be faulted for their high hopes of a better life, to be gained by this improvement on the physical plane."

"Since this Plague, however, there is no denying that without an accompanying advancement in our human evolution, no amount of technology will bring a good and lasting peace to our planet. Our continued improvement, our progress, must be of a non-technological nature. In short, we must become better human beings." Reggie Miller signing off."

                              *   *   *

And then, it happened. It was a simple thing, really. An opportunity to commit a small act of goodness. Nothing very dramatic. Just your ordinary, everyday, now routine, good deed. —

The city, as are most, is crowded. With people, relentlessly pursuing goodness, it's not unusual for a city to have a population of twenty to thirty million people. Crowding is commonplace, but no longer an issue, now that goodness reigns down on the Earth and its people. With a global population of 12 billion people, we have fewer conflicts now than when our population was six billion. Living in close quarters is not a problem anymore. People are polite to a fault. Paradise lost is paradise found.

                              *   *   *

"Reggie Miller reporting on a most unusual current event — The holo-cams on the building in question recorded the entire event. The tragic story unfolds as follows: Two good citizens approach the entrance to a high-rise building. As you can see, the woman is the first to reach the entrance. She reaches for the door, to hold it open for the approaching young man. It's the right thing to do...the good thing to do. It has society's stamp of approval."

"After you," she says, grabbing for the door.

"Not so fast," hurries the young man.

To her great surprise, the young man bursts forward, ahead of her, and grabs the door handle to let her in first. Impolite? Yes. But, he's young and impetuous. She refuses, of course, and urges him to cross the threshold before her.

"After you," she repeats.

"Not a chance," he growls, holding the door. "You first."

As the recording shows, words are exchanged. In this competition to be good, with a crowd surrounding them, who shoved who first will probably never be known. What is known is that within a few minutes of trying to be good, one person struck the other. This seemingly impossible act of violence led to passersby taking sides and a full-scale brawl taking place."

"He hit her. Grab him. Don't let him get away."

"You're nuts. She kicked him first. I saw it. She's the culprit."

"Men don't hit women. End of story."

"That's what you'd like to think."

"Hey, don't you shove me. How dare you?"

"Get off me. What the heck's the matter with you?"

* * *

"How can this be? After 93 years of non-violence, anger has reared its ugly head. It's supposed to be a thing of the past. We're not prepared for this."

"She's right."

"He's right."

"Out of my way, dirt-bag."

"The hell you say."

*   *   *

"The unthinkable is happening — People are intentionally hurting other people. Anger and violence is usurping the day. It doesn't take long for the rest of the media to get wind of what's happening. Word is spreading like wildfire. The astonishing, unobserved truth is out. Everything is not right in paradise. For the first time in anyone's memory, humankind is fighting. And all because of an act of kindness. How can this be?"

*   *   *

"Look at these other holo-cam recordings — See that woman just push that man in front of a car. He's lucky that the car is driverless and stops before running over him"

"You want to take advantage of me? You call that being good? I'm tired of being abused. Take this garbage can and shove it. Now see what you made me do. That broken window is your fault. Don't take advantage of people, especially seniors, and call it good. I'm tired of trying to do the right thing. I want to do something that's right for me."

*   *   *

"Get away from me, you mangy dog. I said get out of here. Don't you growl at me. Take that, and if you come back here, I'll kick the daylights out of you."

*   *   *

"The score is tied, 5 to 5. We're in the top of the 9th. Both teams are playing well. These kids are the best of our little league and we're proud of them. Hey, you, get off the field. Parents aren't allowed on the field. Stop! You can't fight here. Are you both crazy?"

*   *   *

"Lady, you're under arrest. Give me that bat, now."

"He's my husband."

"I don't care who he is. You can't go around hitting people with a baseball bat."

"But, he hit me. He's hit me before. I just can't take it anymore."

"That's all well and good, madam, but you still can't hit him with a bat. Don't you raise that bat to me. Put it down, now. Dammit! Put it down!"

"You shot her. You shot my wife."

"I shot her with sleeper bullets. She'll be fine when she wakes up. Now you, help me get your wife in the back of my car and you get in with her."

"But...but"

"No buts about it. You're both under arrest. Now get in the car before I shoot you, too."

*   *   *

"Watch out! That car is coming this way. There's a man driving that car. He just ran over a bunch of people. He's still going. He's hitting more people. He must be crazy. How can that be? The car is supposed to stop on its own. Someone call Emergency."

*   *   *

"Somebody stop that woman. She's shooting people with a bow and arrow. Stay here, she can't see us behind this wall. I can't believe it. She's killing people right in front of us. She must be out of her mind. This isn't supposed to be happening. Where's a Cop-bot when you need one?"

*   *   *

"Do you see what I see? Is that boat headed towards us? Everybody, get off the dock. Hurry! He's gonna hit it. Run!"

"The boat smashes into the dock and explodes. The boat and all aboard it are blown up in the explosion. Several people who didn't move fast enough to vacate the dock are also engulfed in the flames from the fireball. Nothing like this has happened in anyone's lifetime."

*   *   *

"Reggie Miller reporting from the front lines. Freak accidents and attacks are cropping up everywhere. On closer inspection, they don't seem to be accidents at all. It appears that the underlying truth is people have been competing to do good for years, and lying about it. Confrontations over who did more good than who have been more common than anyone imagined. The realization that we are not as good as we had thought is devastating. Goodness has turned to shame and despair. Anger is emerging as the culprit, even though it hasn't appeared for almost 100 years. It's here, again, and it's infectious."

"Our good leaders are as stunned, as is the populace. Ninety-three years of recent civilization, channeled into good, have turned sour. With success in hand, a peaceful, good, world-society has, paradoxically, turned bad in the process. Somehow, being good has led to being bad. The free expression of honest, inner feelings has been encouraged for decades. It still is. So, what is the justification for this unusual and outrageous behavior?"

* * *

"This just in folks — It's as though people everywhere have just been waiting for a sign to unleash their underlying anger. With lightning speed, individual confrontations are escalating into tribal squabbles. People all around the world are finding tools that can be used as weapons. They are forming groups and going out to find offending groups."

"History is repeating itself. Our violent past is rearing its ugly head again. This is insane. These group engagements are mushrooming into wars that cross old borders. Global violence is cropping up. The world is plunging into utter chaos and global war; all seemingly triggered by two people who became embroiled in a contest to be good. Two goods have added up to one bad. This makes no sense."

"What are we to think? What are we to do? Being abandoned by goodness is unthinkable. If being good is not the goal of civilization, then what is? What will we, what can we, now strive for? If goodness is tainted and not all it's cracked up to be, and so flawed that it's to be avoided at all costs, what is humanity to do?"

"With strokes of good, mankind has painted itself into a bad corner. Cooperation has been undermined, and replaced, by competition. Rudeness and rage have become the new order of the day. Goodness, it seems, is finally proving itself unmanageable and is failing. The devil must surely be smiling. Do the last ninety-three years mean nothing?"

"What to do? What indeed? Will fear rule Earth once again? Do we need another plague? Must a third of us have to die, again? I, for one, hope not."

*   *   *

"Reggie Miller for Channel 3 News here, reporting on these recent angry conflicts. As these battles rage on, only those in their early 100's remembers when this was the norm. They, too, are shocked and disheartened by this violent turn of events. People are angry and they don't even know why. Most have never felt anger before. It seems to have been either non-existent or suppressed. Now that it's bubbled to the surface, we don't know what to do with it. We certainly can't control it."

"Is this new, unwelcome, emotion a picture of our future? Will we return to the global riots of the 21st century? They were caused by shortages of clean water and food. Battles were fought over clean air and the consequences of global warming. This is our history, not our present. None of these conditions exist today. So why the anger? Where does it come from? Are we being set up for a rebirth of the Plague? Do we need a reminder of this magnitude? I think not. We can't be that short-sighted."

*   *   *

"Wait, this just in — Finally, some good news. No need to abandon all hope, yet. At our lowest state, word is beginning to spread of isolated, random acts of kindness. Do you hear that, folks? Kindness. Look at your holo-pads, people. As you can see, the man in the red cap is helping that woman in the green scarf out of her damaged car. A little girl is freeing a dog, caught in a fence. A group of people has formed a chain and is clearing away the rubble from that collapsed building. That man coming out of the water is carrying a woman he just rescued from drowning. These are not signs of the masses succumbing to anger. We have not all strayed from our path of unconditional love. Thank God!"

"Small groups of combatants are walking away from armed conflicts. Name-calling and physical confrontations are wilting away. People are crying tears of joy, not rage. Goodness may not have committed suicide after all. Infrequently at first, then, gaining momentum, random acts of goodness are cropping up, everywhere."

"This wave of anger and violence seems to have been a temporary aberration; an anomaly. Before long, it's clear that people are once again lining up on the side of good. Thank God! Then what was this recent spate of violent conflict about? Was it a reminder of just how fragile our peace is?"

"How to explain? Who knows? Perhaps being good and trying to be good aren't the same thing? Maybe being human means to be imperfect, but with hopes to be better. Perhaps we just have to live with the fact that we can't be good all the time. However, we still need to become better human beings. We need to accept and forgive our imperfections and love ourselves and others anyway."

"Having spent my life examining my grandfather's writings and, at the risk of being repetitious, I have reached the only conclusion possible. We humans are a danger to ourselves and the rest of the planet, not because we're doing something wrong. Our problem is that we're not doing enough."

"We can engineer better bodies. We can make them stronger, disease-resistant bodies. We can even increase our lifespan. With enough time and resources, we can make ourselves immortal. However, until we evolve spiritually, we're doomed to relive the worst of our history."

"Our best and brightest scientists and doctors are not the people best equipped to lead this evolution. Our next evolutionary step is a spiritual one. We need an inner connection to all life. How to achieve this is of paramount importance. Why? Because a species that fails to evolve becomes extinct."

"Our path to survival as a species, is to follow in the footsteps of Gandhi, Jesus, (early) Mohammed, Lao Tsu, Moses, The Buddha, Confucius, Kahlil Ghibran, Mother Theresa, and Martin Luther King Jr."

"Technological breakthroughs and engineered life forms aren't worth a damn if we remain emotional and spiritual basket cases who live in fear of our inner workings. Pogo was right when he said: 'We have met the enemy, and he is us.' We can no longer survive if we continue to let our fear lead us. It is time for a new paradigm."

"If we are to survive as a species, we must turn within to find lasting, inner peace. Otherwise, regardless of our technological successes, we are doomed to beat ourselves into oblivion, time and time again."

"Darwin was right in the 'survival of the fittest', except, in this case, the fittest is not a matter of biology. The fittest are those who love the most. Unconditional love is the key to our survival as a species." The choice between fear and love always has been and always will be ours, and our alone."

"If you read my grandfather, Dave Miller's Pulitzer Prize-winning series on 'The Plague', it's clear that our success as a people rests on whether we strive to bring out the best in ourselves or the worst. In other words, my grandfather was right. We, the people, have to learn to be better human beings; we have to evolve. Our fate as a species is in our hands. Mother nature has made it clear as crystal that we must evolve. The world is not how we find it but how we make it. Maybe, we just have to live as perfectly as we can in an imperfect world."

"Reggie Miller for Channel 3 news, signing off."

The End

Thanks for reading! If you enjoyed this book or found it useful I'd be very grateful if you'd post a short review on Amazon (email copy to me at lubov11971@yahoo.com). Your support really does make a difference and I read all the reviews personally so I can get your feedback and make this book even better. Thanks again for your support

Other Books

by

Don Lubov

The following books by Don Lubov

can be ordered on

Amazon.com

Frosty the Soulman

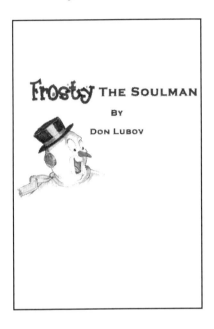

Frosty was born following a snowstorm. He reveled in his youth and basked in the glory of being worshipped by others. Diagnosed as terminal at lunch, he died and was resurrected shortly thereafter and finally became enlightened.

In 612 words, Frosty the Soulman experiences the wonder of creation, the joy of popularity, the pain of abandonment, a cruel death, transcendence and enlightenment.

As a picture book Frosty introduces important concepts to the young reader. His story of life is inspirational in a generic sense that appeals to both secular and religious audiences.

An End to Stress
A Guru's Guide to Inner Peace

"The two most important days in your life are the day you were born and the day you find out why" (M.T.). This book will help you understand the why.

A Guru's Guide to Inner Peace is an informal path, from stress to inner peace. It follows the "Six-Step Path" that has helped thousands of people to live in the present. This guide allows you to accept things as they are, including imperfections in yourself and others.

It guides you to make conscious contact with the non-physical presence within all of us. It encourages you to find your natural gifts and talents and to use them to the best of your abilities. You learn to follow your heart, not your head.

You learn how to make your life your meditation—informal, spontaneous and creative. You become the best you you can be. You are now ripe for a spiritual awakening. You now know that the world is not so much as we find it, but as we make it.

The Side Job

This is the story of Maggie Gomez — an unwed, unskilled mother of a sickly daughter. She lives a hardscrabble life on the underside of Las Vegas. As her daughter's health deteriorates, Maggie's need for money for an operation skyrockets. Maggie was vulnerable and defeated early in life. Her long-suppressed strength blossoms and Maggie becomes "La Femme Nikita". As Maggie gets more involved with her loan shark boss and his crew, her world begins to spiral out of control. Her simultaneous involvement with a gangster and the detective investigating him turns her life into a soap opera of emotions. She must figure out how to escape her underworld life, protect her daughter, and live happily ever after.

Near Death in the Gila National Forest
An Action, Travel, Adventure Personal Growth Quest

Near Death in the
Gila National Forest

*An action, travel, adventure,
personal growth quest*

memoir

by
Don Lubov

When his teaching contract is not renewed, a drug-taking, aimless, university art instructor heads out on a solo backpacking trip across the U.S. Two slick, wealthy drug dealers alter his trip.

It's 1971 and this novice hiker begins a painful series of learning experiences. From a rock concert in the woods, to an invitation to a lynching, to hitching, he plods on, one day at a time, to a purposeless future.

Learning to live in the wild and taking a colorful variety of hitches, he detours to Acapulco, Mexico and a "Big" drug deal. Events beyond his control force him to beat a hasty retreat back to the U.S.

In the midst of wilderness survival in fierce, desert heat and some brief, welcome female companionship, he has a spiritual awakening. Following this event, he gets hopelessly lost in the wild and prepares to die.

Saved from death, he arrives in California, a fitting end to his cross-country trek. His California years include communes, a stabbing, teaching at Stanford and some letdowns. His life lacks direction and meaning.

Finally, 4½ years after leaving the east coast, he senses his purposeful future is in New York. He leaves California, not sadder, but a bit wiser, and heads East to meet his soulmate and a new beginning.

The Writers Bloc Club
Assignments in Prose and Poetry

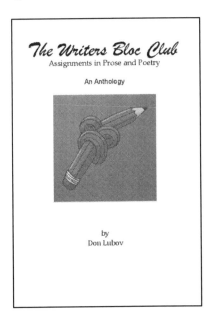

This book contains 62 prose pieces and 52 poems. Most are from assignments from the Writers Bloc Club. A few are optional pieces. The support and instructional critiques of this club have helped improve my writing. The Club also caused me to write on topics I would not have written on otherwise.

Although writing is a solo endeavor, it is immensely helpful to have fellow writers to share and critique my work. I thank them for all their input. This is my first anthology. I expect there will be more in the future.

97494420R00129

Made in the USA
Columbia, SC
18 June 2018